D1234004

1695

WAITING *for* BILLY

and other stories

WAITING *for* BILLY

and other stories

MARTIN HEALY

THE LILLIPUT PRESS
DUBLIN

Copyright © The Estate of Martin Healy, 1998
Foreword © Dermot Healy, 1998

All rights reserved. No part of this publication may be reproduced in any form
or by any means without the prior permission of the publisher.

First published 1998 by THE LILLIPUT PRESS LTD
62-63 Sitric Road, Arbour Hill,Dublin 7, Ireland
e-mail: lilliput@indigo.ie
Web site: http://indigo.ie/~lilliput

A CIP record for this title is available from The British Library.

ISBN 1 901866 26 2

Acknowledgment is due to the editors of the following publications, in which
some of these stories first appeared:
Flaming Arrows, Force 10, the Sligo Champion and The Sunday Tribune.

The Lilliput Press receives financial support from
An Chomhairle Ealaíon / The Arts Council of Ireland

Set in 10.5 on 15 Goudy
Printed in Ireland by ColourBooks Ltd of Baldoyle, Dublin

Contents

Foreword

I first met Martin Healy sometime in '86, after I moved to Sligo. I set up a writing class, later known as the Markievicz writing group, and he was one of the first in.

Nothing finished yet, but foolscap pages filled with handwritten scenes. What was happening in High Street, in the dole queue, back on the farm. Scraps of exact dialogue. Things overheard. What was going on in someone's head. He was always about the town, on his way to the library or off to a session. He lived in a series of small rooms that he kept tidy as a shoebox. The books here, the cassettes there, all lined up neatly.

He was serious. He was often demented with longing. He had a memory that could pick a sentence from a story or novel and keep it there, ready for telling anytime. Even when he was dying he was quoting some line from your work you had long forgotten. There was a great keen generosity at his core, which became overwhelming to see and hear in the last few months of his life. He always read widely, mostly Americans. There is a broad selection of modern literature in Sligo Library because he would order, not only classic works, but books by authors none of us had heard of yet. It was him introduced us to Cormac McCarthy. When we heard him talking of this fellow who wrote about cowboys we thought he had lost it.

From the beginning he was a Carver man. He had the stories off by heart. Things you would have missed, little moments just off to the side. *The mark of the wife's highheels in the snow the day she left,* he'd say, tapping his skull and nodding. He seemed to revel in the minute details – the minor epiphanies. And this attention to detail made it hard for him to finish a story. He kept going over it, all the time checking his vanity, his imagination, his sense of authenticity. Then there was the problem of being intensely aware of all the good literature that was out there. Having it running around in his head. Hearing voices that were not his own. Reading. Reading.

His own generous memory was his chief critic. He endured a great deal of frustration making the selfish leap from reading to writing. He lived in two worlds, one rural and back there in time, the other bang-up-to-date in Sligo town. This was his territory – bachelors living under a mountain who encounter an American lass lost in a storm, a couple waiting on a nephew to arrive in a souped-up Ford. On the one hand there was the world of Carver, the bleak romanticism, the failed relationships, the damaged psyches, the drinking bouts, the love affairs with people passing through. On the other hand there was the hayfield, the bog, the loneliness, the *sean-nós*, the father, the mother, the childhood memories, the fiddle, the clock ticking away.

Out of the Markievicz writers' group emerged *Force 10*, and his first story was published in the magazine. Then he began in earnest. Work away, work away. Sketching out plots, standing his ground, giving up, starting again. Hi buck! Off to another small room to hang up his shirts. The writers' group met weekly and sometimes Martin might try out a new piece orally for the class, but generally his stories arrived behind the scenes to be read in private. First they were handwritten, next they came typed, then when *Force 10* entered the world of the computer Martin took to the Amstrad with a vengeance.

Things began happening for him in the '90s.

He got prizes, he got recognition. He became short-story editor of *Force 10*. He was shaking off his mentors. There is a great photograph of him being kissed by two ladies the day he won two Hennessy awards. He's beaming. He's mad alive.

Looking through these stories you want time for him. He knew what he was at.

Over the last few years he took a great kick of being with Noel Kilgallen in the Lower Rosses. It was from Noel I learned that Martin was sick. Some days, in hangovers, he thought it was to do with the drink. I met him before he went into the hospital and said, Don't worry, that's a hernia. Are you sure? I am. Doctor Healy, as he called me, was wrong. It was cancer of the pancreas. Then I thought when it came to death he might be snivelly. Not at all. He knew her of an old day. He was noble. One night he rang me and said, What happens when I meet the librarian in the sky? Tell him to fuck off.

The morning before he died Brian Leyden went in to see him.

Another day, Martin said, lifting off the blankets.

Sound.

DERMOT HEALY

WAITING *for* BILLY

and other stories

Waiting for Billy

From his seat by the range Paudge Brennan could watch the lane. Without shelter on either side, it rose for half a mile, passed through a tunnel of whitethorns on the ridge, and then dipped away into a more fertile landscape.

Now, though the light was fading beyond the kitchen window, Paudge maintained his vigil gaze. From somewhere out there his nephew Billy would soon explode in a souped-up Ford, come jouncing over the stones, the car beams picking out the limewashed cottage.

Annie sat across from Paudge, a wiry little woman tensed on the edge of her low chair. The silence racing, whipped by the two alarm clocks high on the mantelpiece. Up there, too, was the tinsel-framed Sacred Heart, a few sprigs of wicked holly, and a holy bulb that glowed like a dying ember in the twilit kitchen.

A long hour passed, neither figure having stirred, not even the comfort of a word passing between them. The fire going down, wind sweeping the heathery wilderness abroad. Annie forced a wary eye across the Rayburn and pondered if she should risk a move for turf. A minute later she was up and away to the pantry. As she went she hummed with anxiety.

When she came back in with a dozen twisted sods Paudge barked at her: 'Where are ya goin' with all them turf!'

'Where do you think I'm goin'?'

'Do you want to set the chimly on fire!'

'Ah feck it,' she said.

'Feck what?'

'You're always frettin' about somethin'.'

'I have good cause.'

'If isn't the chimney it's the win'. If it isn't the win' it's the chimney.'

She dumped her load on the back of the range, a vexed and noisy spill.

Seated again she abstractedly flicked turf dust from her new apron. She pushed her tongue against her dentures, the upper plate slipping out for a moment, as if seeking air, before returning with a hollow, sucking sound. Wringing her bluey hands in the valley of her lap she mouthed the words of a special prayer, all the while rotating the thin, gold ring that had long loosed itself from its once-snug grip.

The ticking silence intensified. And still, Paudge gazed beyond the darkened window.

'Any sign?' she asked.

'Nothing.'

'Nothing at all?'

'No.'

There was little to see, nothing but the sweep of the night, and that lonesome spot of light up past the whitethorns – ghost beacon of the Germans who'd recently bought Bartley Dunne's old place.

The wind soughed in the eaves and in the swaying firs. Paudge raised a hand to jerk tight his Sunday cap, as if he were abroad and bared to the elements.

'A bad night.'

'Yes.'

'Win',' he said, 'nothing but win'.'

He'd wear a stone.

Six leaden gongs echoed from the ancient but reliable grandfather clock up in the parlour. Hands flourished crosses, lips tremored the Angelus lines.

Half six ticked down. Paudge looked towards the radio – an old Pye model squatting on a lofty perch – but he didn't rise to turn it on, his hunger for the news and weather forecast keen as ever but not now keen enough. As if to allow the familiar tones of Charles Mitchell into the kitchen would be to surrender, to regularize the night.

Not able to bear the dark a second longer Annie rose abruptly and picked her way over to the light switch. Turning then, feeling exposed by the 75-watt glare, she absently poked a hand deep into the pocket of her Happy Homestead apron. It was empty.

What was I looking for?

'Who's that?' Paudge asked.

'It's only me.'

Blinking against the light, he squirmed within the confines of his armchair and stifled a sigh.

'I must have dozed off,' he said, as casually as he could.

'Aye.'

He gestured to the radio.

'We missed the oul' news.'

'Aye,' Annie replied, 'sure a body gets tired.'

Released at last into a semblance of normality, Annie Brennan lifted the hotplate off the range and lowered sods softly onto its nest of embers.

'I'll make a mouthful,' she ventured. 'It'll warm us.'

'Very good.'

She angled a sharp eye to the front window as she hummed her path to the pantry but resisted the impulse to go and draw the curtains on the night. They sat in to mugs of sweet tea and currant bread on the good tablecloth, patterned with red roses.

After tea Paudge blessed himself mechanically as he upped from the table, replaced his cap and sank into his vigilant's chair. He checked the time and Annie noticed. Christ above make him come, she pleaded, make him come. She gathered the tea things and moped away to the pantry.

She cursed Billy for not turning up, cursed her shadowy God for depriving her, forcing this pitiful dependence on a pup of an in-law who might already be driving to the butt of the wind after women or getting blind drunk in the bars. She knew the same Billy all too well, better than her simple fool of a husband would ever know him.

Embittered, she recalled other occasions when he'd let Paudge down … and the way the poor man always forgave and forgot. Big Billy and his fancy car.

The way he could get round you.

The grin on him as he handed over the poteen – he'd always produce the drop when he wanted to get back into Paudge's good books, back on the track of his nest egg. Too frigging lousy to buy whiskey. The fecker, he'd buy it for himself! Soft Paudge, he could be won with a package of sweets. Saint Jude, please send him this way, if 'twas only for the half hour …

She went back to her chair.

Hearing her, Paudge spoke. 'He'll not make it now I'm afeared,' he said.

'Do you think not.'

'Somethin' must be up.'

'Hah?'

'I'm saying something must be up.'

Eight struck. Paudge's gaze stayed fast on the window.

'Ah feck him, we'll get on without him,' said Annie suddenly.

'What's that you're sayin'?'

'We had to spend enough Christmases on our lone.'

Her husband's gaze dragged away from the glass, settled on her like an accusation. In that paralysing moment, for the connection lasted a mere moment, Annie Brennan felt, stronger than she had ever felt before, crushed by his misery. His eyes bulged.

'Ah he might come,' she said.

'I can't see it,' he said.

He turned back to the widow and she went back to the pantry, just to escape, to suffer her hurt in private. When she returned, Paudge rose sharply.

'Let me help you there,' he said.

'It's alright.'

'No.'

He plucked the turf from the cradle of her arms. She stooped to lift the Christmas cards toppled off the dresser by the pantry draught. Six in total, all flown across the wide Atlantic. She studied them, her oddly girlish face pinched into an expression that could be read as disdain. Aunt and Uncle – the same cold legend on top of each; and inside, the scribbled messages in hands so shockingly unfamiliar. She balanced them, three either side of the decades-old crib, and passed by him.

'The blasted win' is still at it,' he said.

' 'Tis, 'tis.'

'I don't like the win'.'

'No.'

'Never did.'

'It's me that knows that, Paudge.'

'I knew it was comin'.'

'You did.'

'The rooks were on the wires today.'

The mute minutes that followed told Annie that the waiting wasn't over. She eyed the clocks. She searched for words, for diversion, for any small comfort.

'He's comin'! Bechrist, Billy's comin'!' Paudge was up and across to the window, grinning freely despite the arthritic twinge that accompanied his jubilant rising.

'And about time too,' Annie muttered to herself. She remained seated but couldn't hold back her smile of precious relief. God is good.

'Come on, *a grá*, get ready! And bring the bottle up outa the room.'

'Will ya go aisy, you'll give yourself a turn.'

Paudge, still grinning, hastened out to the pantry and unbolted the back door.

The car chugged as far as the byre and halted there, its Volkswagen sputters telling Paudge Brennan it wasn't his nephew.

Annie came out to stand by his side.

'Who is it?'

'Ssh!' said Paudge, and the rise of his hand sent a shudder right through her.

Frank and Joe Shiels, neighbours of Billy, pushed up the stony street in silence. They moved leadenly, they smoked. Frank offered a countryman's honest hand to both Paudge and Annie, nodding as he spoke their names. Then, despite having been cautioned by his brother to wait till they were inside and sitting, he said what he had to say – 'It's about Billy,' he began. '... a bloody tree down on

McGinley's bend ... the poor fella, he couldn't have seen it ... I'm sorry, terrible sorry ...'

Annie gripped her husband's elbow but he pulled away from her.

'Leave him,' advised Joe Shiels. 'Give him a minute to himself.' He then linked Annie inside. Frank stayed out, hands sunk deep in his pockets, his head bowed.

Paudge turned finally. He faintly gestured Frank Shiels ahead of him, into the kitchen where the cards again littered the floor and a bottle of Crested Ten awaited on a bed of blood-red roses.

Could This Be Love?

This messy tale features a dog called Shep, a ruined mongrel whose agony was ended by yours truly. I was asked to do the shooting, of course, but, looking back on it, I reckon I should have refused, should've steered well clear of the whole thing. How was I to know, though, that my act of simple compassion would lead me into such deep water? A man does a good deed and it flies back in his face like shit off a fan. It just doesn't seem fair.

It was about five weeks ago, a balmy Friday evening. I wandered down to the local for a few games of darts and who should I spot, on entering, but Jack Sharkey. This shook me. The Asterisk wasn't one of Jack's haunts; his being there set alarm bells ringing. I thought to turn on my heel but decided, *Fuck it, I'm fed up avoiding him*.

He was supping on his own, the head down, the paws flat on the counter – obviously well loaded. I inflated my lungs and rehearsed a glad smile as I sloped over to him. 'Well if it's not Jack Sharkey,' I cried, slapping his beefy back, buddy-fashion. 'Long time no see.'

He turned heavily in drunken slow motion and grinned. He still has no idea, I thought, rocks of worry lifting from my mind. She never let it slip.

'Malachy,' he said, offering his hand. 'I was told I'd get you here.'

I pulled up a high stool and sat. 'So, Jack,' I said, 'how are tricks?'

'Could be better,' he replied, signalling to Kay.

That's how it started, act two of the shady drama that would involve my pulling the trigger on Shep and lead into other, less terminable, matters.

Christ, it was nothing but a sob story for the next hour. Darts, even a quick game of singles, was out the window because it was a full-time job lending an ear to Sharkey. You should have heard him; it would put years on you.

And all about a fucking mutt. It turned out that Jack's mongrel, Shep, was in a bad way. A horrid sore on the left hind leg, which stank to high Heaven, was the gist of it, but I had to listen to all the peripheral details. The constant squealing of the dog, and the crying of Jack's other half, the lotions and the potions used and useless, the visits to what seemed like every damn quack in the county after the local vet threw in the towel.

By midnight I was pissed, having taken full advantage of Sharkey's rare decency. The pair of us staring into the dregs of our glasses, Kay tidying with the urgency of a bird keen to get away for a bit of pleasure hunting, and not another soul left to lift the gloom.

'You're sure you don't mind?' croaked Jack one final time as we steered each other towards the door.

'Christ, I don't mind,' I said. 'He's your dog, Jack.'

'Shep … Poor Shep,' he lamented. 'And poor Lesley.' And you know what he did then? Hugged me! Spread his heavy arms wide, drew me close as a lover.

Boy, when I think back on it. I can still see him wandering off into the night and saying: 'It has to be done, it's for the best,' and then reeling round to wave me a mute goodbye, rudderless as a man with melted bones.

It was understandable that Jack would plump for me to do the necessary – regardless of the fact that he probably knew nobody else with a rifle. We went back a long way, the two of us. The bold Jack it was who offered me a start when work was anything but plentiful. And a good job, too, I thought at the time. Driving one of his diggers. He took to me in a flash, treated me almost as a son. I wasn't a pro drinker but I was young and green, game to experiment. Off to the pubs he'd drag me, most evenings, no grub eaten or duds changed, lashing into the frothy pints. I was company for him. Nearly all lushes like having someone to chew the fat with. Jack, to be fair, did the bulk of the buying. Probably he was a touch guilty over paying me such shit wages. Even the greediest bastards have areas of weakness.

We all grow up and grow wiser, and the lad who drove that digger quickly copped on that he was being taken for a ride by canny Sharkey. Ten months I stuck it and then: Adios, Jack. We did keep in touch, though. Not that I could ever say I really liked him, but if you spend enough time on the high stool with any man you'll find traces of good. That's a fact.

I got into the masonry line while Jack made more and more brass with the diggers, supped more and more booze. Then, out of the blue, pushing sixty and fat as a frog, what does he do but go and hook himself a jazzy blonde. Invited me to the wedding reception and all, a major do. Jesus, I could not believe it when I saw her. Any fool could figure out she was marrying the dosh but I have to say I envied Sharkey. And I also have to say I welcomed her into my fantasies, pronto. That should have been a warning to me …

I blame Jack. If he hadn't asked me to lay the patio and build that huge prison of a wall round their house I'd never have gone near her.

No, a man doesn't have a clue what he's letting himself in for, until it's too late. What I'm trying to say is I had an involvement with Jack's missus. Seven months going the rounds with her, giving her plenty of what she was missing. Talk about a goer! Aching for it, a veritable cauldron of desire. To this day, I'm not certain if he ever got wind of it but I reckon if he did, then Sharkey is one close operator.

That business with Shep would serve to activate, again, a chapter of our linked lives. The book is still being written. I don't know how it'll end.

The Saturday after I met Jack in the boozer I went over with the rifle, as arranged. Jack was pacing the side lawn as I cruised up, looking for all the world like a first-time papa in the environs of a maternity ward. The clatter of the ramp alerted him; the hands flew out of the pockets and the signalling started – urgent semaphores that screamed: *Quiet! Tread carefully!*

'They're around the back,' he sighed weightily as he led me over the patio, me and my 202. The pair of us peeped round the gable's corner, Jack directly behind me, his fat hands planted on my shoulder blades.

'Look at them,' he droned. 'Wouldn't it break your bloody heart.' And it was a sad sight, I have to admit. There they were beside the pink hydrangeas, Shep looking already dead but audibly moaning his pains, Lesley kneeling beside him like some entranced pilgrim of suburbia. It was then the awful thought struck me and I nearly KO'd Jack with the stock of the rifle as I swung round. 'Does she know? Did you tell her about this?' I demanded, brandishing my sleek instrument of death. He nodded. That's all the stupid bastard could do at that moment, nod. I squeezed his clammy paw and nodded too. The things men do when the pressure hits. I took another peep and let a few seconds float by before I realized how crazy the situation was becoming. 'Get rid of her,' I hissed. Jack, he just stared blankly and I could have sworn I saw the glistening of a tear in his blood-shot left eye. 'Lesley,' I said, pointing wildly. 'Bring her into the house, for Christ's sake.' He drew a rope of air into his wheezy lungs, nodded once more, then wadded off towards the hydrangeas.

The wails out of poor Lesley were dreadful to hear as Jack helped her to her feet and coaxed her away. What happened after was the real tester. Shep's moans climbed a few decibels, fused into a lament of the most awful yelping. I watched as he tried pathetically to drag himself closer to the house. It was almost as if he knew what was about to happen, honest to Christ. The dog is some animal.

I could hear Lesley at it inside; I also thought I heard Jack's impotent pleadings for quiet as I held my head in an attitude of strangely detached listening. I noticed a bold robin hop from the bed of marigolds and settle on the pier of the patio wall. I watched it and it watched back. And still the dog struggled and yelped and still the chorus of grief echoed from the troubled house.

'Come on,' I spurred myself in a harsh whisper.

I picked my way along the gable, then tried to shunt my mind onto an empty track as I went down on my left knee and took aim. I could feel the pulse of blood in my trigger finger, I could hear Lesley.

PING! I fired again, just in case. *PING!*

My hands were trembling as I lowered the rifle and I couldn't even begin to tell you how I felt. The silence was enormous, broad as the sky. I was still frozen in my pose of genuflection when Lesley flew out the back door and made straight for me. I rose quickly and backed away a step – fearing she might lash out, pummel me with her little fists in hysterical abandon.

'Oh, Malachy,' she cried as her tanned arms coiled about me and squeezed hard. I swallowed a big lump of pressure and made to comfort her but the rifle got in the way and I let it drop onto the lawn.

'Sshh, sshh,' I breathed into the perfumed shell of her ear. Jack came on the scene then and folded his heavy arms about us, forged us into a threesome of … of what?

Much shuddering, sshhing, and palming of flesh followed before we pulled apart and all eyes turned to the thing that used to be Shep. Nobody spoke. I heard birds.

'Would you like … would you like me to bury him?' I said, and I'm sure I meant well, but that really drove Lesley off the beam. She was like one of those broken creatures you'd see on the telly, filmed at the scene of some unspeakable carnage. Jack tried to shelter her but she pushed free of his wimpy embrace and again threw herself at me. Can you fucking imagine!

'Stop, Lesley,' I said. I tried to ease away, unpinning her arms gently but firmly, then gripping her wrists; in those moments, it might have looked as if we were disengaging from a messy waltz. I bent, retrieved the rifle.

'Come on, we'll head in,' said Jack in a low, spiritless tone, gesturing us ahead of him, following our close shadows across the unmowed lawn.

Stepping into the cave-like cool of the Sharkey pad, I felt like a burglar returned to the scene of a crime. Deep down, I believed Jack knew nothing; Lesley, in her present state, was the main worry. Bother unhinges people.

As I expected, Jack got the liquor out. Large measures of Martell. It was an earlyish hour to be hitting the hard stuff but, at such times, a drink can help.

Naturally enough, Shep soon became the centre of things and, to hear the pair of them talk, Jack especially, you'd think that dog had had human powers – Jesus, you'd think he'd had superhuman powers. Still, I understood.

Lesley broke into the waterworks now and again but, as the brandy began to hit, she seemed to enter some private zone where a form of solace could be found. Only once did I spot her gazing towards the picture window which overlooked the hydrangeas. 'He's gone,' she muttered. Jack did his own bit by adding: 'Poor Shep.' She was keeping chaotic emotions bottled up and caution told me to be away home before the cork popped.

But Jack wouldn't hear of my leaving. He kept topping up my glass, kept pushing smokes on me – how I didn't go back on the damn things I'll never know. In no time he was starting to buzz. Lesley also. It was more like a celebration than anything else, true as fuck. And Shep still above ground, no doubt already drawing the eye of Mr Carrion Crow.

As the hours floated by I began to feel dangerously relaxed. Food got a mention at some stage but was quickly forgotten. The last wash of the low sun departed the windows, wall lamps were lit, curtains drawn; a sense of illicit intimacy entered the room. And then Lesley slunk across to the stereo – 'I'll play something nice and soft.' I ask you, I frigging ask you! Randy Travis she selected, the laureate of heartbreak. I was half expecting fatso himself to ask her for a waltz because he was high enough for it. Jesus, the way he was downing that liquor. It was getting to him, though, gradually taking its toll. Brandy scuppers the best of them.

In rare moments of clarity I began to suspect he was harbouring revenge, waiting with spider patience for the loose word that would plunge me into his baited web. Even the most placid of men can turn nasty when a betrayal visits his house. My only hope was that he'd flake out. But what then?

We kept supping, our chatter wobbled along, we found lots to laugh at.

Sometime, I became foggily aware of Lesley's eyes snuggling into me, all dreamy intensity. I gaped into my Martell, rolled it about the tumbler and swallowed a stiff gulp. Later, while Jack was over at the booze cabinet, I found myself nibbling at the hook of her gaze. She jetted smoke from the side of her mouth, nodded almost imperceptibly and smiled a knowing smile. Like Lauren Bacall smouldering in the shadows of a piano bar.

I needed air, space. Up I got and off to the refuge of the Sharkeys' loo.

I thought I looked oddly sober in the bathroom mirror; I moved in real close, like a lad about to attack a blackhead. After dabbing at my lawless mop for a few abstracted seconds I straightened and cocked an ear: silence abroad. Without any prompt of will, my hand then reached out to pick some of Lesley's things off the glass shelf. I caressed them, sniffed. I turned to stare at the partly open shower curtain, dazed by a flash of memory. We were in there, myself and Lesley, hard at it. I could almost hear her deep moans riding on the steam, feel her claws raking my shoulders. Stop it, I cautioned. Christ's sake! In that sobering moment, I swore I'd steer clear of her. And I meant it. I did, I honestly meant it. You must believe me.

Sighing heavily, I flushed the toilet a second time, took a first squint in the mirror, pinched the bridge of my beaked nose, and then back out to the sozzled Sharkeys.

The door jamb got in my way as I floated into the smoky silence. Whatever the mirror said, I was pissed as the proverbial newt.

The rest of the night – well, I can't really say much about it. That's me and booze. I'm like the marathon runners who hit this phantom barrier they call the wall. Except with me there's no getting round it, no second wind. Attempts at later recall yield little, leaving me marooned in the wasteland of tortuous conjecture.

I did, unfortunately, have some flashbacks. One of them featured a saucy Lesley slouched low on the couch, slow-sucking her thumb, delighting in my mongrel discomfiture. Jack was out for a leak then, pissing like a mule no doubt. Another event I would remember with appalling clarity was my getting sick. Or *trying* to get sick, I should

27

say. Kneeling, my paws on the rim of the toilet bowl, sweat, the dry heaves bucking in the pit of my belly; and Jack planted on the edge of the bath, smoking, contented as Mr Buddha, wheezing: 'Get it up … get it up …' Say what you like, the drink is a bad job.

I haven't a clue what time it was but I do remember actually leaving the house. The wash of night air clearing a space where memory might live.

'Mind, Malachy, that the boys don't bag you!' Jack's voice booming free, locationless, as I wandered down the crazy-paving path and fumbled for the car keys. I forced my head round but he was already back inside, the *thunk* of the door stout as a shot in my brain, the silence of suburbia total.

Driving off I saw only the wiper blades lazily sweeping the dew from the windscreen and showing me the way to go, the same dew that also kissed the pink hydrangeas, that kissed Shep's snout as he lay in his last stillness, that kissed everything open and bared to the innocent July sky.

I was in rough shape when I woke. The head, it's always the head. At least it was a Sunday so I could have a lie-in – a dubious comfort. I believe it is wiser to force yourself out of bed and get on with your day, don't give the inner demons a chance to poke at memory. But I was too fucked to rise.

I started to sweat as I floundered back through the fog of the Sharkeys' night. Bulbs of shabby detail lit up. My heart was going like the clappers.

And then I thought of the rifle.

'Motherafuck!' I cried, flying from the bed and down the stairs to check the alcove. No rifle. A dire scenario instantly presented itself. A loaded gun in a house where all is not well, drink, a jealous husband beating the truth from his wife … then *PING!* A drop of piss leaked into my Y-fronts.

That's the demons when they cut loose. Specialists in horror.

Later, back in the clammy bed, I could laugh at my panic over the rifle. Sharkey was no psycho; and anyway the thing wasn't loaded, me sticking in just what I'd used. I didn't laugh, though. I wasn't out of the fog yet.

I drifted into a dead sleep, only to be shocked awake by a hellish drone.

Baldy Don Jones, my nosey neighbour. The bastard would have to pick today. I couldn't help but picture him shaving his miserable patch, one shoulder strap of the pressed dungarees hanging loose, his bullet head cocked in an attitude of careful verge-watching. You'd think it was Centre Court at fucking Wimbledon. I lay rigid as a pole for a few head-splitting minutes, then ejected from the bed and scurried downstairs in search of Solpadeine.

The day passed: that's about the best I can say for it. I was coming round a bit by evening time, watching the box with the volume turned down, when the doorbell rang. I ignored it. It rang again. I still ignored it. It rang a third time. Enough.

The first thing I saw was the cocked eye of a rifle. 'Oh … Lesley.' I tried to sound casual. 'Come in, come on in.'

'You left this behind,' she smiled, handing me the 202. She was dolled up. She looked the fucking biz.

'So,' I said, when we were sitting.

'So,' she said.

'How is everything since?'

She gazed at me blankly, and just when I thought she wasn't going to answer she shrugged and said, 'So-so. You know yourself.'

I cleared my throat and nodded, then stared fixedly at the box.

'How are you?' she asked.

'Coming round slowly,' I replied. 'The head's not the best.'

'I can imagine. And you got sick and all, poor thing.'

'Hmmm. Sorry about that.' I looked at her. 'Hope I didn't …?'

'Make a mess? No! Sure you couldn't get anything up. I mean, 'twas a dry vomit you had,' she added rapidly, flustered by the double entendre.

'I'm not used to spirits.'

'I know, I know that, Malachy. Don't be worrying about it.'

'I was, to tell you the truth.'

'No need. It's over now, no harm done.'

'Sound.'

'I quite enjoyed it, actually. Took my mind off things.'

'Jesus, we must have drank a lot,' I said then, grinning a natural grin. I was relaxing, I suppose. After all, we were only talking. Just talking.

'That's Jack,' she sighed, taking a packet of Marlboro from her handbag, fishing one out and cracking open her gold-plated lighter.

There was damn-all affection in her voice, not to mention love.

'It's hit him hard, hit both of you hard,' I said, squirming visibly in my chair. 'Losing the poor dog like that,' I added with absurd solemnity.

'The dog,' she said: an appalling chuckle.

'Mmm, that's it.' I felt pressure rooting in my jaws.

'Malachy, look at me,' she said. 'Look at me,' she insisted, and finally I did look. 'Jack's a drunk, dog or no dog.'

'He likes a few drinks surely,' I conceded, 'but I don't know about him being a drunk.'

'He's a drunk,' said Lesley again with such stern conviction I began to think she herself had a few on board. There was a void of silence then. I could sense her eyes on me and could imagine what class of a look was in them. I started to squirm again.

'I'm really grateful for all you did, Malachy. You know – with the rifle and that,' she explained awkwardly. A screen of smoke wafted over to me. I inhaled it. I said nothing.

·'It was my idea to get you,' she continued. 'We could have used the vet but …'

'I know. I know.' I was talking again. 'It's not easy.'

'No.' She sighed heavily. 'Jack would let the poor thing go on suffering for ever. Can't make decisions, that's his problem. One of his problems.'

'He tries his best, I suppose.'

'What's the point in waiting? Should've been done long ago.'

'Still, nobody likes to see a dog put down.'

'Shep,' she hissed. 'You know, that's all he ever talked about. Shep-this-Shep-that-Shep-Shep-Shep. Malachy! Are you listening to me?'

'I am,' I said. 'I'm listening, I hear you.'

She blew a smoke ring and watched it float up and away from her painted lips before resuming her diatribe. 'That dog was half blind from the first day I laid eyes on him. Down in the pub, that's where he bought him. Where else! There's a mug in every pub.'

'Ahhh, a dog is a special class of an animal all the same,' I said, the statement slipping out easily, encouraging me to go on. 'Any dog – even a half-blind one. They're often the kindest.'

'I know that,' she sighed, bending instinctively across to press the cap of my locked knee. She withdrew her hand in slow motion, eyeing me all the while. 'I know that …' she said again, lower now, in a voice coloured by something I took to be shame. I let her digest this fugitive emotion; I wondered what it meant; I wondered if she'd say more.

'Oh, Malachy,' she said, 'if you only knew all I went through these past months. All the nights I sat staring out that damn window.'

I heard her start to sniffle. 'Well,' I consoled, 'at least he won't be suffering any more.' The sniffling grew louder; it grew so loud I couldn't just ignore it. 'Come on, Lesley, don't be getting yourself annoyed.'

'I'm fed up!' Sobs shook her asunder.

'Sshh, it's all right.'

'I'm sorry about this, Malachy. Sorry.'

'You're grand,' I said, eyeing her furtively. 'A good cry helps.'

There followed a long minute of tick-tock silence. I could hear her sobs trail off gradually; I could hear the irritatingly regular snipping of Don Jones' shears; I could hear the jumbled echoes of local children at play.

'Where's the man himself?' I asked casually, knowing full well but, for some nebulous reason, wanting it confirmed. She didn't answer, didn't even shrug, just gazed at me and absently kneaded her ball of tear-soaked tissue. I nodded. I swallowed with a degree of difficulty.

She continued to gaze and the gaze soon got to me. I knew what those gazes can do, how they can pull a man in, disarm him completely. But I couldn't slip it. Or maybe I didn't want to slip it.

My heart began to flutter when she finally spoke. The room felt airless.

'You were always gentle ... understanding,' she said, composed once again, flickering a smile. 'That was one of the things I liked about you.' She started to say more but, instead, sighed and absently tugged her skirt down an inch.

I stared into the hushed television. I angled my wrist and stole a check at the hour.

'You keep the place neat,' she said in an abstracted yet intimate voice; then she pushed from her chair and went on walkabout.

'Mmmm, I suppose I do,' I said, taking a good deep look at her, now that her back was turned. She picked a darts trophy off the sideboard and blew dust away; she fingered the spines of my few books. I thought of fat Jack, probably bombed in the The Blind Piper, and again checked my watch.

I felt myself stiffen as she turned and moved towards me. Slow, assured.

'Mal-a-chy,' she said, three drawn-out syllables. 'Look at me. Please.'

I forced my eyes up to meet hers. Every sinew in my body was tensed. She played her fingers along my chin, a feather lick, then smiled her Lesley smile and floated back to her chair. When she crossed her legs, her skirt rode high and she let it be.

Silence again took root. Baldy Jones had turned his sprinkler on.

'Say something, Malachy,' Lesley pleaded presently, that opening 'say' elongated with need. She lit a fresh Marlboro and puffed at it edgily.

'I don't know what to say,' I said. And I honestly didn't.

'Say anything; say what's on your mind. It's not like we're strangers.'

'I know,' I said defensively. 'But ... but that was in the past.'

'Forget the past,' she said. And then she said, in an absurdly affronted tone, 'Jesus, Malachy, I only came over to return the blasted gun!'

'Okay,' I said. 'And I'm grateful,' I added quickly, feeling a sting in my jaws as I plunged myself deeper into the charade.

She smirked. I didn't eye her but I knew she was smirking. I just knew.

'Must pop up to the loo,' she said, casual as you like. That lilty tone.

My eyes stayed glued to her all the way out the door, then I checked my watch and saw it was moving on for closing time. I rose and crossed to the box, absently turned up the volume, lowered it again, flicked through the channels and then stared, zombie-like, into the uncharted middle distance.

She seemed to be talking ages up there but eventually the toilet flushed, swept me back to my chair. I tried to look relaxed. I craved a cigarette.

Don't do it, a little voice whispered in my head. *Think of Sharkey.*

33

The sight of her slinking through the doorway blitzed the little voice.

'Memories,' she said hazily. 'It brings it all back.'

I stared at the box.

'Do you ever think about me ... about us? Do you, Malachy?'

I pinched the bridge of my nose. It was a straight question and it had to be answered.

'I suppose I do,' I said. 'Sometimes. Now and again.'

Her eyes livened and she smiled, some veil of sadness seeming to lift.

'You're so tense,' she said, fishing a Marlboro out but deciding, at the last moment, not to light up. 'You've been tense ever since I got here.'

'Me? Tense?' I said. 'No, I'm fine. It's just ... just a bit ...'

'A bit what?' she crooned.

'Strange. It's just a bit strange.'

'You mean me being here like this and ...?'

I nodded.

'Would you prefer me to go?'

I had to say 'yes' or 'no'; I said neither. I could feel my heart going.

'I didn't only come over to return the gun, Malachy,' she continued, her voice dragging. 'And you know that.'

I nodded again.

'Come on,' she smiled. 'It's Lesley you're talking to now. You know very well what I mean. What about last night?' she tailed off, meaningfully.

'Last night?'

'Yes, last night. Don't tell me you don't remember.'

'We were all drunk,' I snapped, my mind fired into instant panic.

'So we were,' she said.

'Listen, Lesley,' I cut in. I didn't get to say any more because she had upped from her chair and was advancing. She knelt in front of me, sought my hands and brought them to her opened face and then down to her breasts. All thereafter was frenzied and free.

We lay side by side on the floor, our hearts fast as competing clocks. Lesley's arm napped on my chest, at peace on its bed of sweated hair.

When she moved to rise I felt myself wishing she didn't have to.

She turned onto her elbow and studied me. I kept my eyes on the ceiling.

She then eased astride me, the action so natural, so ... affectionate. I saw doubt in her eyes, also a yearning for reassurance. I began to caress her face – as if her features were Braille. She quickly misread my intent. Her head swooned back and notes of gaspy breath broke from the pit of her bared throat. Something toppled, hit by a flailing leg (I later saw it was the ashtray, the tall one that Lesley had been using) and this minor punctuation was enough to break the spell and set ringing a bell of alarm in my brain. 'Stop,' I said.

I rose onto shaky legs, searched amongst our scatter of shed clothes for my Y-fronts. I coaxed them on. The same with the trousers and T-shirt, the socks and the shoes. Dressing had never felt so fucking complex.

I looked everywhere but at Lesley.

'Malachy,' I heard her say, 'please don't be upset.' I heard the stud of her skirt snapping shut, also the scrape of a zip, but I didn't turn.

I had to say something, but I wasn't at all sure what I wanted to say. When I turned finally Lesley was doing up the shiny buttons of her blouse, and appearing none too concerned, it should be said. She bowed her tousled head for a long, private moment, as if balanced on the tightrope of a decision; then she crossed to take hold of my hands.

'Are you sorry about this?' she said. 'Please say. I have to know.'

I pulled free of her eyes and her hands, I wandered away a few steps and righted the ashtray. The weatherman was on the box, pointing at a map with his cane.

'I don't know,' I said. 'Are you sorry?'

She eased up behind me and wrapped her arms about my waist. 'What do you think?' she said. I said nothing. I realized, then, that I seemed to have spent half the fucking night saying nothing.

'You had better be going now, Lesley,' I said. 'It's getting late.'

'I know,' she said. 'I know.' She held on, touched her lips to the nape of my neck, squeezed my waist so suddenly and urgently she might have been trying to dislodge a bone from my throat. Only then did she disengage, all brisk and businesslike.

She lifted her bag, got her brush out and raked at her hair. I picked a few butts off the floor and absently checked that my zip was shut.

'Do you want a lift home?' I heard myself say as I forced my head round.

'I've the car,' she said. 'Hardly walked all that way with a big gun!'

She put her brush away, lit a smoke and gazed reflectively into the high spaces of the room. Cobweb territory. The clock counted down the seconds.

'Right,' she said after a bit; her tone reflected confidence in a decision reached. 'I'll head, Malachy.' She settled her eyes on me, a last, deep look; she nodded, almost imperceptibly. 'See you soon.' She traced her index finger along the bridge of my nose, as if placing a territorial mark, and then off she strode, her hips rocking, her hair glistening, her head held high.

'See you,' I muttered into the void of perfumed silence she left behind.

It was wrong and I shouldn't have allowed it to happen. And I couldn't even blame booze, not that being drunk would've excused it either. I cursed the dog.

Yet when Lesley rang my bell three evenings later, I ushered her in with the barely controlled eagerness of a junkie welcoming his dealer. I missed her and that's the truth. Something had changed. Changed, I mean, from the time I was building the wall at Sharkey's and poking indoors on the q.t. I sensed it might have been my heart threatening to get involved. And that I needed like a hole in the head. She was married, is married. And to a half friend of mine. Watch yourself, I cautioned.

Anyway, to get back to that Wednesday evening and Lesley's visit without the ruse of a rifle. I made coffee. We sipped it. The telly was on and she asked me to switch channels so she could watch *Birds of a Feather*. She had no real interest in it, I'm sure, but no matter. When the ads came on she went out to the kitchen to wash our cups. I soon followed. She was looking for a tea cloth as I crept close and slid my arms around her. Nothing was said. I kissed her neck, right on the spot where she liked it to be kissed. She pressed her bum into me and steered my hands inside her jumper. 'Come on, we'll go upstairs,' I said. No. She wanted it right there – and quick.

The cups trembled on the draining board as we fucked rapidly. Up against the sink isn't the most comfortable site for sex but there's a time for it and that was our time. We held each other long after the cups fell silent, held each other until we, too, had ceased trembling.

There was no consequent awkwardness. We lounged on the couch, up close, my arm draped over her shoulders. We were fully clothed, having only taken time earlier to remove the immediate obstacles. Lesley's smoke clouded up into my nostrils but I didn't feel an urge for a drag. That said something good about my state. It should also have said I ought to exercise caution, for the intimacy we were then sharing was new – new, at least, to me. Call it a sense, or some other interior word, but I felt, as the minutes passed without talk or the need of talk, that a level of control had deserted me.

And I liked the feeling. And I believed Lesley was experiencing a similar feeling. People don't talk when the mood is such. Like they're afraid it's a spell, something that a single word might break. So it was with us.

But, of course, we had to talk eventually and we did talk. A bit stiffly at first but we hacked it, we got onto smoother ground. Jack wasn't spoken of, or Shep, or the night of our previous joust. I can't really remember what we did talk about. Suffice to say that it didn't unnerve us any.

I made more coffee, used the same cups. We smiled a lot at each other. I was aware that I hadn't smiled so much for a long time. It was so strange, the way the evening was turning out. Everything perfect. But was it real? – the question I would ask myself later. Later didn't, just then, exist.

The news came on. We had no heed in that, it was too much of a jump from our current state. I channel-surfed, then hit the off button. I suggested we go out for a drink, someplace quiet. Lesley loved the idea. We stood, all buzzed up for the road. I took her hand in mine.

We kissed. A real gentle kiss, not the sort we were used to. Like we were tasting and valuing each other for the first time. We hugged. And that, too, felt good. Even better than the kissing. But we returned to the kissing and before long we were easing, as if through a haze of bliss, towards the stairs.

We made love. Slow, slow love. Savouring the lazy tempo of it. Making love with our eyes, it felt like, for our eyes were linked all through.

Even nearing the highest peak of pleasure, a strange calmness prevailed. Lesley's eyes flickered and glazed and I felt her coming and we came and came and we were both smiling and then wrapping about each other in a swoon. And though I wasn't conscious of it, it was during those moments that the seed of another question I would ask myself later became planted.

Lesley left around twelve. I stayed up till the small hours, wondering.

Sunday, she called again. And she's still calling. It's getting awkward, so it is. The thing is going too smoothly, there's too much swooning. One of these nights she's going to say she loves me, I just know it, and what do I say? It's not exactly a line a man can wriggle his way round.

If I close my eyes now I can see her. Savouring a last cigarette before leaving. The way she steers it in slow motion to her lips and inhales ever so quietly, as if fearful of disturbing the pattern of her mood. Her wistful smile when she catches me studying her. Her sigh.

She does love me. I half wish I was fooling myself but I know I'm not.

Looking back on our earlier involvement, I do believe that she may have hinted at such feelings even then. Maybe that's why I put up the shutters. Don't forget she was freshly married. Christ's sake, what was I supposed to do? And, more importantly, what am I supposed to do now?

Could this be love? I asked myself that question, and I still ask it. No day or night passes that I don't ask it. Imagine getting to forty-five and being none the fucking wiser on heart matters. I even practised saying the words aloud, planted before the mirror and staring at myself like a prick.

I love you, Lesley … I think I'm falling in love, Lesley … Could this be love, Lesley? I did, no word of a lie. But I remained at a loss.

Jack. Just think of the poor bastard. Lesley says he suspects nothing as he's too busy exercising his elbow, and I believe her. He is a drunk. Damn it, he was never anything else. Why doesn't he stay at home more? Take her out for meals and that, treat her right. If there is a blame anywhere it's with Sharkey himself.

But then why do I feel this constant shadow of guilt? A guilt that sees me floundering through the mornings, confused and diminished.

I'm back on the smokes. Four small words – spoken over the phone – did the damage. Let me explain. Lesley left a few behind one night and I put them by, thought no more about it. But I was always conscious of where exactly I'd stored them. You never know when an emergency will crop up; I was glad to know they were within reach.

The phone rings about an hour and a half ago. There is this spring in my step as I go to answer it, I know it'll be herself. Yes, yes, I admit it, it gives me a buzz when she calls, and a bigger buzz if she says she'll be over later. That's the way it goes. Anyway, I sit down and get settled and lift the receiver. We share a few minutes of small talk. I grin a fair bit because she slips in the odd saucy morsel. Jack is away on tour again, she can say what she likes. She'll be over inside two hours. Can't make it any sooner, the exterminator man is calling. Several suitable – no, unsuitable – gibes suggest themselves but I hold them in. He's still her husband, fat Jack. And then, just as I'm expecting to hear her usual crooned *Byee!*, she goes all silent. I know something is coming. My grin fades. Thoughts of having a shower and sprucing myself up for her arrival are no more. She's silent for mere seconds but it still counts. Silence is dodgy. I have the receiver pressed against my ear. I hear her intake of breath, then I hear the line: 'We need to talk.' My immediate response is an intake of breath, deeper even that Lesley's. 'Hold on,' I say. 'I'll be back in a sec.' I stride to the emergency store and get out the Marlboro. No thought involved, I just do it. Matches … 'Hold on!' I shout out to the hall, to the waiting Lesley. I think of the ornamental lighter on the mantelpiece. I try it. 'Light, fuck ya, light,' I urge, flicking like crazy. A flame finally appears, a pathetic fuck of a thing. I'm away. Puff-puff-puff. *We need to talk.* I'm silently mouthing the line as I go back to the phone, my step revealingly slowed. I take a long drag before I lift the receiver. 'Sorry about that,' I say. She has hung up.

I'm smoking Major now, my old coffin nails. Just back in from getting them. I asked in the shop for twenty, then said forty, and finally took sixty. Not a good sign, I fear. She'll twig it, too, she'll read panic behind the nicotine fall.

We need to talk. I know what that means, I'm trying to get ready for it. It's a serious one but not half as hairy as the thought that struck me an hour ago as I wandered round the corner to the shop. I thought of my rifle being called for again, its target human and beer-bellied. *Shep II*, as it might be titled in your local cinema. The fucking things that machete into our skulls when the mind is under siege. Those demons, they never sleep.

I'm making a list. A mental list, like. Cross off what I can, leave a question mark after the others.

1: Sharkey hasn't copped the truth. If he had done, herself wouldn't be so buzzy on the phone. All the saucy stuff, and then the clear focus about the exterminator calling. No. Cross Jack off.

2: She wants us to go public. Go for a drink in some boozer where neither of us is known; or maybe an odd jaunt to a hotel, stay over. She has had time for invention, she wouldn't be short of a story to feed Jack. Hmmm, I could handle that. No. 2 out of the way.

3: She intends to come clean with Jack. ?

4: She has already decided to leave him. ?

5: She wants to move in here. ?

6: She wants us to start a new life elsewhere. ?

That's six possibilities. There's more, too, I'd say. Christ, of course there's more. How about her having decided to dump me? It could happen. I could be as blind as Jack. The Jacks of this world have the dosh, a woman will ponder long and hard before turning her back on it.

No. I could make lists till the cows come home but, come the moment when Lesley walks in that door, they'd mean nothing. It'll be just her and me, our eyes meeting, no place to hide. The eyes, they never lie.

I'll go along with her, whatever she wants. Play it by ear. She just said we need to talk. That's fair. Nothing need be decided tonight, we'll just talk. Talk. It sounds so fucking easy. Fuck it, either I love Lesley or I don't. 'I love you, Lesley.' Jesus, I'm smiling, all of a sudden. 'I love you. I love you.' It feels good to say it. I'll say it. I will, I'll say it. If it comes to the crunch, I'll say it.

It'll work out. It'll be fine. I am not used to it, that's all. Too long putting the shutters up. Even when I was building that wall at Sharkey's I think I may have been in love with Lesley. There, I've admitted it. Fuck's sake, what class of a man am I at all?

We will talk. It'll be a relief to talk.

Zzz-zzz! She's here, and the place a fog of smoke. Keep calm, just keep calm. Let her in.

Straying

S he was dropping, at last, towards the ocean bed of sleep when the sudden cry snagged her, broke her dive. It was late, the dead of night. Frost drawing patterns on the moonlit window, the outer world quiet as the temperature fell to minus ten. The high ground of Tubber gripped, glinting.

Her heart pounded as she waited for the cry to echo again. *Wuu-arrhhh!* It wasn't the banshee, thank God, just the lows of a cow in the byre. *Wuu-arrhhh!* The bought-in Friesian who was chained, night and day, because of her straying. 'One deadly bad buy,' himself had often said. 'She'd rove to the butt of the wind. Won't settle.'

Poor thing, Sheila thought, feeling for the beast. Missed her home place, anxious to get back there. Cattle had nature, more of it than many of their owners if the truth be told. Money, modern farming was all about money.

She turned away from her snoring husband. Nothing worrying that man. He didn't know how well off he was.

She pondered getting up and warming a drop of milk. It was good, a mug of hot milk. Calming. But she decided against it, didn't want to risk waking John. He had a tough day ahead of him tomorrow, scattering the piles of manure in the top field.

Growing more agitated by the minute, she found herself imagining how he'd react. A fit of grumbling, that'd be it. No stime of natural understanding. Share a bag of flour with a man and your eye'll be opened! Her mother's old saying had a lot in it, daft and all as she was. Life had learned her.

She stared across at the pale void of window, listening for the Friesian to again howl against the dark, against her chain. One more creature unable to find ease in the dead hours. *Wuu-arrhhh!*

In her seven married months, Sheila had suffered many sleepless nights. She couldn't reason why, and she certainly couldn't blame John. He was a good man, hard-working and sober, even kind in his own reluctant way. The bother lay deep within.

The prospect of the coming morning now weighed on her. Lack of sleep made her contrary, like a bag of weasels. Himself wouldn't pass any heed; or, at least, pretend not to. Gulp down his breakfast and then out quick to attack the manure. Easier to toil with a graip than to face a red-eyed wife across the table. She often wondered if other men were like that and in her heart she suspected they were. Closed, frightened by any hint of intimacy, of opening up. A different breed altogether.

John mumbled and stirred, his drawers-clad behind pushing warm against her hip; then he settled again, his snores evening out. That was one of the things she most valued in being married: the actual physicality of him beside her, the sense of safety it offered. Worse to be alone in an empty house, nervous of roaming gangs out for plunder. Or ghosts.

But there wasn't much else, really, with regard to the bed. Intercourse, when it did occur, which was seldom, wasn't at all what she'd imagined. Big John, he could be so blunt and maddened, grunting as he drove into her, his urgency reeling her brain. Squeezing her fleet-ingly and turning to the wall when he'd finished, not one word out of him.

In her spinster days she had given little thought to carnal mat-ters – the chances of lying with a man being, then, remote as the stars. Yet when she started seeing the shy bachelor, especially that first night they'd waltzed at the parish social, her senses were shock-ingly quick in responding to his touch. The feel of his settled hand, spanning the small of her back as they clumsily circled, made her yearn for more. Later, awake in her own bed, she pondered further and bolder contact. What must intercourse feel like? Would pain be mixed in with whatever pleasure there was? If he asked, and she took him, would he be demanding, turn to her often?

Wuu-arrhhh! The bloody cow was at it again.

Sheila had scant sympathy for the beast any more, each ragged cry winding tighter the clock of her nerves. Sighing, she tossed onto her back and then round to face her husband's nebulous bulk. The movement caused him to smack his lips briefly, punctuating the line of his snores. She sighed again.

Had she been braver, or he a different class of man, she would have woken him. Even a crude coupling might see her over the bridge to sleep. Such an hour wasn't for sex, though. There was a time for everything.

She roosted her hand on the sturdy bone of his hip, a tense hand, a claw. Christ, it was as if she were back in Dublin in that honey-moon bed, balanced on the knife edge of their newness.

Wynn's Hotel, long favoured by journeyers from the west. Near the train station, not too posh. They'd squirmed through the revolv-ing doors on the dot of nine, nervous as hounds. The welcoming smile of the young lassie on reception, the guest book gaping open. John mumbling: 'Sign it you.' The pen trembling as Sheila wrote John and Sheila Donnelly, suddenly unsure if Donnelly had one L or two. Sheila Donnelly. A giddy sensation in the pit of her stomach as she saw the name in runny ink.

Steak dinners in the murmuring restaurant, then drinks in a quiet corner of the lounge. Sherry for Sheila, bottled Harp for John. Things went grand, once they got used to the place. And not a sinner knew them – that was the beauty of it. They would have enough gawking to put up with back in Tubber.

Imagining every eye on them when they finally ventured upstairs. Sitting on the edge of the bed for awhile, small-talking about aspects of the room. So awkward in those loaded moments, both wishing for the dark.

'A handy yoke,' grinned John sheepishly when Sheila pulled the cord above the headboard – the signal for him to extinguish the more exposing light.

They undressed, back to back, and twisted into their nightwear, trying so hard to feel at ease. The bed, a blank page, waited to be filled.

Neither slept well. City traffic moaned and moaned into the small hours.

The next day they took in the Spring Show, as planned. John wanted to get a price on hay-bobs: make sure Friel, the local supplier, wouldn't rob him. Sheila loved the whole spectacle, the sense of being away. Thanks be to God, they were getting on powerful.

That night John drank more that his customary few bottles and, later, the obstacle of intercourse was negotiated – in a fashion. Again, Sheila got no right rest, but she was pleased that her husband did. His level snores said he was at peace in his dreams; she held him close, her mind's eye roaming.

Sheila Donnelly, née McFadden, withdrew her hand and rolled onto her back. 'John,' she said in an abstracted tone, enunciating the word as if its echo were lost to her, as if she were trying to regain its slipped meaning. John slept on. The frost patterns on the mooned window grew in complexity.

Sometime later, driven towards escape, she left the prison of her bed.

Just as her soles touched the lino, the cow's bawl gashed the membrane of night and sent a chill right through her. She stood rigid for a long moment and then hastened to the door. Three paces in the dark; she knew them well.

A trace of warmth still lingered in the kitchen, though the open door of the Stanley showed only a grave of ash. She sat, laid her head back and planted her feet against the end of the range. No snores here, no shrill tick-tocks; the silence total.

Within minutes she was dead to the world. She dreamt she was in bed, in a lovely warm bed. Sun beaming through the window, time to rise. She tried to leave the bed but something was restraining her. Her head, she couldn't free her head. She struggled and strained – then she jolted awake and gasped the chilly air. Eyes wide, she gaped all about the kitchen, its plan seeming, for a while, utterly foreign to her. 'Jesus,' she whispered.

If himself were to see her now. Would he hold her close and offer calming words of reassurance? Or would he just stare, mute and fearful, thinking to himself that there was, after all, a 'drop of the mother' in her?

'Jesus,' she whispered again, shuddering from head to toe. No one to turn to, nowhere to go. She was trapped, and she knew it.

The tide of history swept Sheila with it as she stood and began to pace the floor. Hugging herself against the cold, thinking back, tormented by truth.

She couldn't have luck. Plunging into marriage before Bridie, her mother, was settled in her grave. Small wonder her mind was astray.

Birdy – the nickname. Mad Birdy on the twisted tongues. Aye, she knew how people saw things but the bad word couldn't touch them then. Sheila smiled wistfully as she recalled simpler days, hearing again Birdy's cackled laugh filling the cottage kitchen. Home, that cosy nest. Just the two of them for so long. Doing her best for her doting mother, shielding her from the hand of the stranger. And wasn't it right? Lord God, wasn't it only natural? But they wouldn't help. Oh no, Maura and Ellie were far too busy with their own grand lives. Dump her into a home quick as you'd wink.

Sheila sat on one of the hard chairs at the table, weakened by grievance. Her razory elbow anchored on the oilcloth, her chin in her numbed hands.

Landed their pick of men but sure they had the prize jobs. Easy to find suitable takes with the salaries of the Bank of Ireland behind them. Fecked off then and lived like ladies. Ohhh, but youse were quick to forget!

Birdy's burial flashed forward, as it so often did. Maura's gaze settling on her as the first cakes of dauby clay clunked onto the coffin lid. A look so blank yet penetrating, loaded with awareness. As if her smug sister were stretching a plank of guilt across the chasm of the grave. Or maybe it was something else entirely? Maybe she was thinking to herself: *Don't you start harbouring blame, Sheila, you made your own bed and sacrificed your chances by lying in it. I defy you to say different.* Damn her, the painted bitch!

Impaled on the hook of that cool gaze now, Sheila was forced to confront the most unpalatable of truths. Yes, she could've got out. No one asked her to play nurse. Four honours in the Leaving, the future was open to her. And the years she'd wasted in penny-ha'penny jobs in town, shops and the like, simply to be near home. Dancing to Birdy's every beck and call.

Almost immediately, her mind shunted onto the track which had led to John Donnelly. Their token courtship; the two spins into Sligo – just to traipse around the streets like fools; him showing her his house and stock, coaxing her to pat the fat bull; and then putting his bank-book on display. Looking back on it, she couldn't understand how she had strayed off her life's path so casually. Big, quiet John, scrimping and slaving down the years within a mile of her door. Never gave him the second thought – until the evening he called round with a Mass card. *I'm sorry for your trouble, Sheila.* That's when it started. Wynn's Hotel on top of her in a flash.

Fear, it must have been fear, she told herself. Fear of ending her days alone in the cottage, neither chick nor child for company. Hmmm, maybe she did wise? The past simmered, relentless.

'Bitches!' she hissed, screwing her bony fists into the oilcloth.

Her thoughts turned to the Christian citizens of Tubber. She felt herself smile, a smile of defiance, of vicious pride. They thought she'd missed the boat, never imagined she would capture John Donnelly. Aye, she'd shown them. They wouldn't be pitying her now that she was queen of eighty acres. Pity – the cheek of them! And the way they'd eyed her that day at the funeral. Poor Sheila on her lone now – all because of mad Birdy. Turning a biteen queer herself, too. God love her.

Such desperate musings drained her. She thought to sneak back to bed but, instead, she planted her arms on the oilcloth and allowed her head to sink onto them. She drifted, drifted, the cloak of sleep again enveloping her.

The wan wash of dawn was creeping through the kitchen window when Ignatius Lynch flew past on his way to work, the din from his two-stroke Yamaha loud as a chainsaw slicing through Tubber. Guided by quick instinct Sheila rose and stared towards the bedroom. Listening, listening. She tiptoed forward, her teeth clenched against chattering. She was careful to avoid the two loose floorboards, and get through the door without drawing a creak from that either. She thanked God for these merciful silences and for the racket of young Lynch's bike, thanked Him the instant she slipped under the blankets, safely returned.

She had got back in before himself rose. Little else mattered, just then.

Her abandoned half of the bed was cold but the simple sensation of lying there, flat on her back, was more satisfying in those relief-filled moments than any imaginable luxury. Birdy must have been looking down on her.

Just after half-eight the alarm clock sprung into life and seemed to jangle for an age before John's big hand pounced on it. He let a few minutes pass, as usual, reluctant to leave his cocoon of warmth. Sheila could imagine his eyes fixed on the ceiling, the plans for the day taking trusty root.

'Are you awake?' he said quietly.

'I am.'

'More frost I'm thinking. Another skinner.'

Then he sighed heavily and said: 'Better hop out, I suppose.'

She watched him head up to the kitchen where his clothes were cosy in the hot-press. The skein of hair dangling limp over his left ear – his senses not yet alert enough to sweep it up and settle it across his baldness; his arse fat and wobbly inside his drawers. She was still smiling, long after he had moved from her eye. Such a full and unshadowed feeling, it amazed her.

She rolled into the centre of the bed and drew the blankets close. Savour the warmth for a while. Himself'd be gone foddering – she had a half hour. Her body pleaded for sleep but she denied it its wish. I'll make him a fry, she thought. Have some meself, too. Again, she felt the gift of a smile.

As she crossed to the window, drawn by the glittery light, the chill of the room's air made her shiver. Frost screened the glass. She thumbed it, meaning to thaw a porthole through which she might view the nature of the morning. It was on the outside, the frost, all on the outside, yet she continued to rub with her thumb. Sun was out there also, trying to burn off the night's complex weavings, trying to shine in. She had one thought, just the one thought: *Himself will get a noble day scattering the manure.*

A Burst Blister

It was a crisp April morning, just gone half seven, when I ran over to the cowhouse where my father was milking. The air smelled different, the world felt fresher at this hour. Everything was still as a stone.

Today was the big day, the day I would go to the bog for the first time. This was even better than getting up at six o'clock on winter mornings and going out with flashlamps to round up the cattle for the walk to the fair. This was her, my first chance to show my worth.

How often I had listened to them talk about the big bog in Carnagulcha. The *meitheals* of men all over the place, and the fires for cooking on, and the grand taste everything had, and the race to see who would cut the most and wheel the fastest.

And stopping in Charlie Durcan's bar for a mineral on the way home.

It was all swimming in my head as I flew into the cowhouse. Carnagulcha!

The name had a certain ring to it. Secret as my granny's songs.

I was nine, then. My brother, Tom, was thirteen and had often been to the bog before.

He strolled about the street, whistling what he thought was a tune but was just a thin stupid noise. The hands buried in the pockets and him kicking stones casually, trying to show me he knew it all – that bog was nothing new to *him*. I didn't care, I'd surprise him once we got there.

My oldest brother, Jack, who was eighteen, was helping with the milking. He was under the strawberry cow; she was fierce quiet and would let anyone draw her. The other three were dangerous, especially the red one – she'd send you flying off the stool as quick as she'd look at you. My father was the boy could handle the kickers. He had a special way of scratching their bellies and talking to them.

I drove them out after the milking. They were slow to go, looking round, kinda nosey, as if they realized it was earlier than normal. Her ladyship, the red one, tossed her head so I gave her a mighty crack of the stick. My father smiled and said, 'Good man, Brian, that's the stuff for her.' I was my father's favourite – at least I think I was.

We always talked a lot. I suppose, mostly, it was him talking and me listening. He told me plenty of things. Stories about when he was young, bits about his own father.

We hit for the bog at half eight. My mother had the tea stuff packed in a box that had pictures of oranges on the sides. She used extra-strong twine from Auntie Mary's parcels to tie it on the carrier of my father's Raleigh bicycle. As she watched us leave, I noticed she was smiling funnily – much like the very first morning I went to school. She waved and I waved back. Then she disappeared into the kitchen, rubbing her hands in her apron.

There were only two bicycles in the house so my father had to manage me on the crossbar of his, while Jack brought Tom on the carrier of the other one – it was my mother's so there was no crossbar. My arse started to feel sore from all the bumping as we hurried out the stony lane but once we hit the tar everything was grand.

Paudie Scanlon was driving in his cows as we passed by his gate. He gave a big happy shout and tipped his hat back like a cowboy. His fields were next to ours, and, at hay time, the race between us was hectic. We always won because the poor fella had no help. He never married but he was mighty handy at building cocks.

We seemed to travel a bit faster after seeing Paudie. Like we were ready to beat him at bog, too.

We passed through Dunbeg at exactly nine on the chapel clock. There was a man in a blue coat carrying a tray of bread into Cassidy's shop. I wondered if we could stop for ice-cream – you could get massive wafers in there for a tanner. My father just zoomed by it in an awful rush – I don't think he even saw man or shop.

I was kinda surprised later on when he decided to walk a windy hill that didn't seem too steep to me. He was puffing hard, I realized then, and had done hardly any talking for a while. Jack stood on the pedals, kept going full blast. 'Come on, you're failing,' Tom shouted back at us. I felt like giving him a good kick, straight into the you-know-where.

A few TVO tractors, with wheelbarrows roped to the draw-bar, farted past us. The drivers waved and my father waved back. No hello or anything, just a steady wave. I suppose they were black strangers.

'Nearly there, Brian, *a grá* – get ready to make a wish.' We turned left, onto a grey lane which seemed to snake on forever through the endless bog. I was speechless with wonder and couldn't think of anything to wish for. There wasn't a house or a right tree anywhere, just lonely flatness, with little squares of black here and there, which I knew to be fresh turf.

After about a mile we slowed to a halt. My arse was stiff as a poker, my legs all pins and needles. 'Where's ours, Daddy?' I asked excitedly.

'On down this way, son,' he pointed, crossing a low ditch and following a path that I could barely make out. Grey, like the lane, but spongy.

'Can I wheel it?' I asked, and he let me take the bicycle. It was high and awkward, nearly impossible to balance.

'Big baby,' Tom muttered, loud enough for me to hear. I gave him a dirty look and kept going, careful not to spill the box of tea things.

'Lord, but Meehan is the early bird,' my father commented, gazing across the bog. I followed his eye and spotted the lone figure, black as a rock.

'Sure, Meehan is always here earlier than anyone,' Tom said – to let me know I was the newcomer and knew nothing. I squeezed the handlebars tight, having to listen again to his stupid, straight whistle.

The sun was getting a bit warmer now, the sky a lovely blue – as blue as the sea had been that day Uncle Frank brought us all down to Strandhill. Jack took the lemonade bottle of milk and sunk it in sticky mud, with just the neck up, then he pulled the barrows and *sleáns* from their hiding place in the hollow. My father stripped off his jacket and jumper, rolled up his shirt sleeves. I did the same and chanced a look at Tom to see his arms were as thin and white as mine. He didn't notice, being too busy throwing shapes and spitting on his hands like a grown-up.

There was a long stretch of bank cleaned and ready. My father nicked the side of it at great speed and then paced to the middle, where he opened a cut. He threw the first, dryish sods up onto the bank and I raced over to collect them. I intended to make sure I spread for my father – let Tom and Jack do as they like. I think he was glad about this arrangement because he gave me a wink.

'Right, boys. In the name of the three Devines from Keash, we'll start,' he said, and I felt ten feet tall by the shafts of my wheelbarrow.

The top spit was very stringy and 'twas hard to keep the sods from falling off as I flew out the spreadground, one eye on the load, the other on Tom. Nobody said anything but there was a bit of a race on. The second spit was wetter, and by the third we were down to the real McCoy – grand dark turf, soapy as anything. I put twenty-six on each time – three rows of eight and two across the top. It was a heavy push but I wouldn't give in.

My father and Jack gabbed a good bit as they swung the *sleáns* but I was too busy concentrating on the catching. Tom was silent, too – there was no whistling now! I noticed his face was already blackened where a sod had struck him. Jack was a wild cutter. You could see the difference, plain as day. My father's half was dead level, his sods even as pounds of butter; Jack's was rough, not much better than a pig rooting. Any fool would know he was raw at the work.

Although he was awkward, Jack cut as fast as my father for the first three spit. I was mad, seeing this, but I said he'd never last the day. We'd cut him out long before the evening and then I'd let a shout. I had often heard my father use that line – 'cut him out' – when he was talking about great men from the old days. If there were a line of cutters working on a stretch of bank and one slowed, he'd be in the others' way and have to step down. This would be an awful shame, he'd be the talk of the place afterwards.

We stopped for tea around one o'clock. I was glad of the break because my hands were getting a bit sore and looked as if they might blister. We all washed in a boghole, using fists of mucky mud as soap.

Tom broke into his whistling again, as if he were fresh as a daisy. I knew by the cut of him, though, that he was getting enough of it – I just hoped I'd last the day!

Jack made a fire out of dry clods and twists of newspaper. It lit grand and in no time the kettle was singing. We dangled our legs over a heathery bank and ate our fill of the sandwiches my mother had prepared. Slices of rasher between thick cuts of soda bread – greasy and lovely. I picked the fat bits off and threw them away; I noticed Tom was doing the same but my father and Jack ate like horses, all the time staring silently across the flatness. I'd never had such an appetite, *never*. Only then did I believe the stories I'd heard about grub tasting better on the bog.

'Think will ya stick the day, Brianeen?' my father suddenly asked. I said I would, no bother, and jumped to my feet to show my mettle.

There were a lot of men about now, mostly in twos. You could hear faint voices drifting over, like the smoke from the fires which were everywhere. It was like nothing I ever saw before, like another world. It was hard to imagine ordinary places like school even existed. I thought grown-ups must surely have a great time.

We rested for half an hour. Nobody said much, just listened to the broad silence and gazed at the tiny, distant figures here and there. I did a bit of gazing, too, as I presumed that was the way real bogmen acted. A couple of crows came out of nowhere and hovered above us, watching for scraps.

When my father put on his cap it was time to rise.

By three o'clock they were down five spit and Jack was still staying tight with my father. I flew in and out of the spreadground, not worrying about any sods I lost. Once, my hands slipped off the shafts and I ended up with my face buried in the damn turf. Tom let a mighty cheer out of him and I felt awful.

Jack had stripped to his vest now, his balled shirt flung away into the hollow. Out of the side of my eye I noticed his muscles bulging and, soon, I got to wondering if he could be as strong as my father. Or stronger?

'Come on, boys, we'll cut ye out,' Jack said suddenly. Half laughing.

'Don't break Dunne's *sleán* anyway,' my father answered, and I thought he didn't sound too happy. I squinted round and saw Jack's sods were huge but there was neither shape nor make to them. I was going to say something but didn't.

When the seventh spit was cut we stopped for more tea. My father slipped a bit when he was climbing up onto the bank and I gave him a hand. He smiled kinda strangely and ruffled my hair.

'We'll bottom it this evening,' Tom said. Talking big. The head of him!

'No bother,' agreed Jack, marching into the hollow for his shirt.

The grub tasted just as sweet as before. We polished everything off, not a crumb left, and settled to rest for a while. I noticed how Jack lay flat on his back and closed his eyes. The big sods had got the better of him, I thought, and boy was I glad. We'll cut them out yet, I said to myself, and the blister on my right hand didn't seem so sore anymore.

My father's pocket watch clicked open, sang shut. He glanced sideways as Jack rose, smart as a hound, and again peeled off his shirt. I felt an odd tightness somewhere in the botttom of my stomach.

There was hardly any talk as the eighth and ninth spits were being cut. They were down very deep in the bog now and it was getting harder to throw the sods up. Jack was keeping a close eye on my father and I knew he was doing his level best to cut him out. I put extra sods on the barrow, piled them as high as I could, raced faster, but still he kept gaining ground.

Then, for the first time all day, I noticed the odd sod slipping off my father's *sleán*. Also, he never took a second to look upwards, just kept on flinging as fast as he could – the crown of his peaked cap was all I could see. Once or twice, a sod caught me hard in the face but there was another zooming up before I had time to wipe the stain away.

Coming to the end of the tenth spit they were still neck and neck. 'Come on, boys, keep your chains up,' Jack said, copying a line my father often used in fun at the hay. Tom said something, too, but I didn't give a damn about him.

On the eleventh spit I knew for sure that my father was done. A lot of his sods hit the side of the steep bank and landed right back at his feet. The odd time he did look up at me his eyes seemed far away and almost sad. His face was pure red and his cap was twisted at an odd angle.

Jack finished first but he didn't brag or cheer or anything; neither did Tom, to be fair. When my father finally got to the end he climbed up into the hollow and took off his cap and ran it over his brow and then said to Jack: 'Cut one more off it all, you; that'd be twelve, we'll do with that. Meself and Brian'll clean the far bank, get it ready for tomorrow.' His voice was real normal, same as ever, but we all knew what had happened.

I flung the barrow aside and couldn't look at him for a few seconds. My blister had burst earlier, without me noticing it, but I didn't care about that now.

At seven o'clock we hid the barrows and *sleáns* in the hollow and got ready for home. My father turned to look back across the spread we had blackened and said: 'That was one mighty day's work. Brianeen, you're a noble man for the bog.' He was smiling but it wasn't like the smile in the morning, when we'd passed Paudie Scanlon's gate. I smiled, too, forced myself.

He cycled a lot slower than on the way up, and Jack stayed close beside him all the way – although he could have flown on ahead, I'm certain. They talked a good bit about different things but I wasn't really listening.

There was a huge crowd in Durcan's bar when we went in, all looking like bogmen. My father and Jack took bottles of beer, myself and Tom had orange juice. We sat on a form away on our own in the corner and once or twice I thought I saw a hint of my father's normal smile returning. I think a part of him was proud of Jack.

We passed through Dunbeg at twenty past eight and finally got back on the road I knew. My father patted my head and I twisted on the hard bar, gazed up into his face. I wondered if he might have let Jack best him – surely nobody could top my father at anything? Then, as we were freewheeling down the windy brae by the graveyard, I remembered a story he had told me once, while I was picking potatoes after him. It was about when he was young, like Jack, and his own father and himself were digging together. He'd dug his heart out to better his father and finally, in the evening, he did put him off the ridge. His exact words rang in my head then, echoey as bells: *He sunk the spade in the ridge and said I'm a done man and then he headed for the house.*

I felt fierce sad and alone for a few seconds, and I hated Jack even more, but then I remembered how my father finished that story by saying he never regretted anything as much.

The Lion Sleeps Tonight

I'll call him Frank. He's in enough bother, the poor bastard, without the likes of me exposing him. Anyway, this is more about myself than any Frank.

Right. It's half ten in the morning, the town is getting busy, the pubs are opening their doors. He's half a street away when I spot him. Lots of people footing it in the space between us but Frank stands out. Something kind of familiar about him, a focus I recognize. As we draw nearer to each other I get the feeling he has sussed me – same as I have sussed him. I steel myself. Thirty paces apart now, twenty, ten … We're locked onto a collision course. We meet. We stop. Dead casual, like two mates on for chewing the fat. Horses, football, whatever. But we don't say a damn word, this is the thing. Frank, he takes a last drag out of his butt, dumps it, gawks at the shoppers, faces me again, looks me straight in the eye. And still no word. There's a fair whiff of whiskey off him. He must have been at it early, probably in Lourdes. Down the docks at seven, knocking for the cure.

He stares once more at the human traffic, a detached witness. It feels like ages we're standing there, our lights fixed on red, before he finally speaks. 'You heading for one?' he says, says in such a neutral tone I hear statement rather than question. He purses his lips as I waver, then shrugs and continues on his way. I'm caught. I turn and say: 'Wait.'

Drive a man nuts it would, cooped up here. I've rented a box to pass the time but there's only so much Oprah Winfrey, quizzes and soaps a head can handle. Who watches that fucking crap anyway? No, a bedsit's the pits. Okay for students and the like, they can hack it. Take the gang in this tenement warren, Christ they're having a ball. Doors banging at all hours, music blaring, the later sounds of sex. Riding like rabbits. Supping, too; cider and those new long-neck lagers. Such a buzz off them as they zoom up and down the stairs, their faces flushed with – well, I suppose with what my own was flushed with once upon a time.

No point in this feeling-sorry-for-myself moan. I made my own bed.

Went for a bit of a wander into the country this morning. A wander, that's what it was. Big difference between a wander and a walk. It's an absolute bastard having to always opt for the quiet paths, steering clear of temptation and risk. So much to be wary of: that concentrated aroma of alcohol while passing pubs; bumping into a mate on the jag; *fleadhs*; even the thought of going to a funeral – funerals are the diciest of the lot. The steadiest of drinkers let rip after funerals.

Couldn't, though, avoid the Frank man that May morning. A head-on smash.

Lowe's was nearly empty when we sloped through the creaky doors. A few old boys guarding half-ones and bottled chasers, a business type nibbling nuts and scanning the paper. Not so bad, I thought. Quiet. As if it would make a blind bit of difference how many were there. Or who.

Frank asked me what I'd have and I told him and he ordered and Mick Lowe interrupted his shining of glasses to look after us. Lager I'd opted for, though 'opted' is probably the wrong word. My eye just happened to land on the Harp tap, simple as that. I was jittery. Four weeks without putting a drop to my lips and now this.

So. Frank hands me the pint, nods stiffly, avoids eye contact. That same man has seen it all. Straight off, in case my hand decides to shake, I sip the frothy head – and a wee bit more. Then I have a good swallow, a couple of inches of cool lager. It tastes exactly as I expected.

We parked ourselves away back at the end, well clear of the glinty light spearing through the window. I was settled in no time. Wild how quick that happens. You can come into a pub in bits, hardly able to handle coins, yet get two or three quick drinks in and you're on top of it.

Ask the boozer. They'll all vouch for the reliability of the cure.

Nearly five. *Dallas* will be on soon. A rerun of an eighties' series – but, to me, it's all new. Soaps, I can assure you, weren't high on my agenda in those days.

No demons spiking at that gent, JR. Still, one never can say. Every man jack harbours a touch of mystery, some secret need.

You should see the range of people that attend the meetings. All types, from the student to the priest to the old dames with the blue-rinse heads. Each with their own story. And don't think they're exaggerating, piling on the drama. No way, José, not in AA. If you want fiction go to the library.

Myself, I haven't yet stood up to unload. To be honest, I don't see much point. I know what I had and what I hadn't, what I lost and how I lost it; I can't imagine telling it will help. There's a limit to what's gainable.

> *In the jungle, the mighty jungle, the lion sleeps tonight!*
> *In the jungle, the mighty jungle, the li-on sleeps to-night!*

They're back, the gang downstairs. In the door, and straight on with the stereo. They must have that frigging song on the brain. Fair play to them, though, for making hay while they can. They'll hit storm soon enough.

Take me and Frank now, and plenty like us. What wouldn't we give to have another crack at it?

We hit for Lowe's first, that's right. Two we had there, maybe three. Talk was scarce. It was early, remember. Frank said we'd talked horses one morning in Lourdes. I accepted this was possible. The early houses are full of Franks.

Leaving there I left my bit of shopping behind but missed it before we'd gone twenty yards. Back in for the bag, sharp Mick already beating a path across the flags with it. 'Youse forgot this,' he croaked, peering at me over his spectacles. I thanked him and split.

The Quail was our next stop, a sort of tricky compromise. See, it wasn't every place we'd be welcome. It's only when you start touring with someone like Frank, a man with a similar history, that you're forced to confront the wreckage of your own doings. To be straight about it, half the pubs in the town were out of bounds to one or both of us. So it seemed anyway, judging by the number of blanks we drew before hitting on the Quail. It was a weighty truth to have on board but we coaxed a laugh from it nonetheless. You have to be able to laugh. Without that you're fucked.

Soon enough I discovered that Frank wasn't too flush in the cash department. Not to worry. I had plenty in the pocket, as usual. Even during that maiden month on the dry I always carried large notes when venturing out to the shop. An ominous precaution, yet it brought a kind of comfort.

Course, I realize now that wily Frank understood the dependability of my finances the moment he spotted me on the street. Probably heard I'd got a lump when I was let go from the mill. Or maybe I was too free with it some time in Lourdes. What odds. I never minded buying for a man stuck, never.

Right, we're in the Quail. A grand wee name for an awful dive. Remember being there one day, summer, the door thrown open, and in limps this half-blind mongrel, cocks his leg, sprinkles the face of the broken jukebox and off out with him, nobody blinking an eye. Still, 'twas as good as the Ritz to the likes of us. You can't drink posh interiors.

Lager could be dodgy here so I have a bottle of Stag and then join Frank on the whiskey. There's a fair crowd, mute drinkers mostly, a few already well lit and on for debate. Ordinary men doggedly working their individual ways towards higher ground, just getting on with it. Noon hasn't come yet. There will be lots to time for talk later, the very air will buzz.

Not a sound in the house now. Friday, they're all away home. Crammed on to provincial buses to Donegal and Galway with their washing. There'll be no lion sleeping tonight. Two long days before I'll hear a key scraping into the front door's lock, voices, feet pounding the stairs. Christmas coming soon, that'll be a lot worse. A man on his own at Christmas knows the meaning of isolation. Especially a man not too long dry. Staring like a zombie at the box or out the window at a greyness of tenement roofing, chimneys smoking or not smoking, maybe a lone pigeon perched and preening. I think staring must lend itself to the condition of aloneness – or should I put that the other way round? Whatever.

Take mirrors for instance. There's a big one over my mantelpiece and hardly an hour goes by without it drawing me. I just stand before

it, rooted, and stare. Maybe it's the lack of company, the depriva-
tion, a need to see a human face – even if it's only my own. Or
maybe I'm simply driven to confront the history that a stilled eyeball can reflect, to keep facing it, facing the pain. My eyes are pits,
have been for a long time; I could look into them for ever and see
nothing.

It's no wonder I hit the bed early most nights, not that the dark
offers much comfort. An odd judder from the fridge; a sudden echo
ghosting from the heart of the town – shrill and unnerving. It's one
awful way to have to live.

At least I'm not out. Or supping secretly here. That's something.

When they got into the swing of things the Quail men proved to be
a rough crew. Frank's doing. He stuck his oar in, and you can't get
away with that anywhere. Cool it, I kept telling him, keep her
steady, but I was as well talking to the wall. See, Frank, I find he's
the type who goes fierce high on the whiskey – which is all very fine
if he had a placid nature. But no, I have to say he's a pure dread.
Goading-goading-goading, the eye on fire. Can't help it, torn inside.
Anyway, we had to cut our stick abruptly. 'Get your mate out of
here,' the bar lad whispered to me, and I knew his advice was sound.
Jesus, the place had gone dead quiet. When a hush comes over a pub
like that you can be sure an explosion is ticking down. Not surpris-
ingly, Frank wasn't keen on retreat. He's small, jockey weight, but he
didn't let that discourage him. Said he'd go when he was ready, said
he didn't give a fuck for any white man. I managed to quieten him,
don't ask me how.

Led him through the silence, away out the door, remembered my
bag and all.

Heading down the street, he drew me close and, composed as you
like, he said: 'No one crosses me.' I nodded, let it go. Some nasty line
in his jaw, a viciousness. Boyos like that are capable of anything.

We wandered for a while, squinting into the sun. I felt grand. A calming fuzziness in my head, the echoes of traffic and voices slightly muted. The day was opening its arms to me; we'd soon be aloft at another counter.

'What about Leahy's?' said Frank then, pausing at the post office corner to light up, catching my eye with a question-mark hook. 'How are you fixed there?' I said there was no problem. He jigged his shoulders with relief.

We continued on, saluted the odd person we knew, never once stopped.

Suddenly, so sudden it wrenches the breath right out of me, my whiskeyed cocoon ruptures. This girl, see, she breezes past us, and, holy Jesus, I'm convinced it's Lily. The spitting image of her. I stop dead, turn in dazed slow motion. 'What's up?' I hear Frank ask, his voice sounding distant and toneless. I've no response. I've been mistaken and I realize this. My only child's in Darwin, thirteen thousand miles away; she's not here. Yet still I continue gaping at those red pigtails bobbing amidst the mill of people. Frank drags at me. 'C'mon, c'mon,' he says, 'leave the young ones alone.' I face him, meet his eye. 'My daughter ...' I begin, but then I run out of words. He seems to understand. He nods heavily, gives my arm a fleeting squeeze. It's a feeble gesture but I appreciate it. I return his nod.

We resume our trek to Leahy's; silent, step for step.

Funny how, the lower our ebb, the more we nurture our losses. Remember one night I came back here, plastered, and where did I end up but outside the door of the young lassie in the attic bedsit. Niamh. Tap-tap, a beardy lad opens it, goes to shut it in my face. But Niamh, she stops him, says it's okay it's only Brendan, tentatively ushers me in. God love her she's a wee saint. So, I'm in there, plonked into a sofa, this beardy, her boyfriend I suppose, puffing on a roll-up and pacing about. Didn't want me intruding, and could you blame him? Coffee, Niamh is giving me a mug of black coffee, but I shake my head, reach for her free hand instead. Fair play to her she doesn't panic, just leaves the coffee aside, hunkers down and lets me take her hand. I squeeze it and caress it, sandwich it between my numbed palms. Imagine.

I'm staring at her, holding on to that hand as if in those fogged moments it's the one thing in the whole world saving me from toppling over the edge. I'm aching to talk, to tell her everything, but I can't concentrate a single thought. In a remote sort of way I'm aware that my head is rocking, that my mouth is gaping open, wordless; and all I can do is press her fragile hand and continue to gape, try to hold her plaited pigtails in clean focus. They hang limply down her front – ropes of blood.

I woke in my own space, trapped in a mire of remorse and vague longing.

I lash into the whiskey in Leahy's. Frank doesn't mention the incident on the street but I know from the veiling of his eyes that he realizes it has followed us. It's rooted solid outside the door of the snug, a boulder too large to roll aside. He still has heart, Frank. I'm glad of his company.

I make many journeys to the counter. Nora, the stoic granny who runs the place, is glued to the racing on the television, small wagers keeping her smoking steadily. We're safe enough in here, left to our own devices.

Time passes. We enter lulls where nothing is said for maybe twenty minutes; we climb out of those troughs and talk ourselves back into heavy silence.

I dip into my bag and we pick a bit. A few slices of corned beef.

As the day slides imperceptibly into evening, the odd couple pushes open the door of the snug – after a spot of privacy. None enter. But then, at maybe nine or so, the door moans open again and this lone woman stands her ground, fills the entrance with naked purpose. Instantly, I grasp it's Frank's missus. She's staring scornfully at him – it is as if I'm not even there. Her stare is one that I well recognize, the stare of a woman who's located her man after a lengthy search. This'll be ugly, I fear. Her lips tremble for a few seconds before she lets fly.

'Look at the state of you!' She's entitled to be annoyed, of course, but I've seen men in worse shape.

She sits down with a sigh – a sigh both fragile and pained. What now? I think to escape to the jacks but she's in my way. Fuck.

'Well? Are you coming home?' Her voice is speeding, a kind of manic energy to it. I steal a glance at Frank and see he's concentrating only on his smoking.

'Go on, go with her,' I find myself saying.

'Stay out of it,' he replies. I advise him again, calmly, knowing he might blow; even as I'm speaking I'm also imagining Nora, cocking her keen ear. He does blow.

'I told you to butt out!' he warns. I feel him glaring at me. I lift my glass and stare into it. The poor woman stands, points her finger.

'Right,' she says. 'Keep at it so! Drink your brains out! Only don't come crawling back when this binge fin –'

Frank crashes his fist down, bringing silence, sending the change on the table whirling – he has heard all he is prepared to hear. They're eyeball to eyeball now; the snug is bloated with pressure. A few seconds later I hear this: 'I'm leaving. I can't take any more.' Her tone is so resigned, so pitifully colourless, it's as if she is making one final promise to her private self. Whatever they mean to Frank, her words hit home to me. She's beyond idle threats. I inhale stiffly and inch my gaze up from the table but by then she has already fled, the door swinging, moaning, in her wake.

Experience now tells me to head for the counter, the jacks, anywhere – give the man breathing space for a few minutes. There's nothing I can say, nothing he'll want to hear. But when I make to rise I feel anchored to the bench, trapped by the chains of a relived moment from my own history.

I turn to Frank. He seems to be staring at a knot in the ancient wood of the snug wall, rigid as a man of stone. I have no idea what he's thinking, or if he's thinking. He shrugs free of his trance and absently drains his glass. Our eyes meet. For maybe six seconds they stay locked and then, in a fashion, we get back to where we were. We can't stop, certainly not now.

I'm still half tight when I wake in my narrow bed. My head is throbbing. I check my watch: gone seven. All is silent, above and below. Gradually, the map of the previous day takes shape. *Shit!* My heart is speeding, must have drunk a load of whiskey. I start to sweat. I fling the covers back. I try to work saliva about my parched mouth. I check my watch again. I leave the bed, mope to the window and stare out over the town's rooftops. I suck in air and turn away. I check in my trousers' pockets: a few coins. I look to the chest of drawers. I hesitate, for I understand that if I take those two paces forward, pull out the top drawer, peel a couple of twenties from my wallet, I'll be away to Lourdes like a shot.

Jesus, I want to give in. It's easier. One hour there and the shadows, the guilt, would shift. Today would merge with yesterday, tomorrow wouldn't exist. I'd feel that calming fuzziness, I wouldn't have to think at all.

I pull on my trousers, my jumper. I stare out over the rooftops again. Just stay a short while. A few drinks to settle me. I won't rim it, no.

I'm trembling as I give free rein to these old deceptions.

And then I hear sounds from the attic: Niamh is up and about.

The girl on yesterday's pavement, she ghosts back into my mind.

I listen to Niamh's stirrings; I stare at the ceiling, a stare that reaches all the way to Darwin, Australia. Time stops. I feel racked with a father's shame.

The top drawer creaks as I tug it open and the creak causes me to wince.

I'm so tense, you'd think I was robbing, or dealing with a bomb. I peel off a twenty, gnaw at my upper lip, peel off a second twenty. I slide the cash into my pocket and exhale quietly as I ease the drawer shut. It's then the mirror hooks me. I absently brush some dust away and confront the image that is me. It tells me nothing I don't already know.

Dizziness hits as I flop onto the edge of the bed, a hint of nausea too.

I bend for my socks and shoes. Pop music echoes from somewhere in the maze of the house. Low, so low I might be imagining it. I scrape a hand through my hair, check my watch and say: 'Right.'

But five minutes later I'm still sitting, hunched, my chin in my hands.

Something has stalled me. I could be in Lourdes and ordering now but I'm not. I'm here, more or less sober, I'm safe. I imagine swallowing a large vodka, a dash of lime in it. Or a gin. Frank might be down there, we could tour for a while later. Maybe back a few horses on the way.

I sigh shakily. It's torture, this indecision.

'You heading for one?' I hear Frank's voice, I see his boozer's gaze reading me as the shoppers drift past. Four weeks, I try to focus on those four dry weeks. I was doing grand. The head was improving, I was starting to sleep better. Didn't need AA or nothing.

Without thought, without even being aware of doing it, I loosen from my hunched pose and creep back into the bed. Instantly, I feel this massive load of pressure lifting. Okay, just stay as I am. Don't think. I hug myself. Don't think. The morning'll pass. Okay.

I close my eyes. Soon, I see Frank's missus, her pointing finger. I hear his fist crashing onto the table. I see the girl who wasn't Lily. I see so much, I see nothing at all. I re-enter the void that's mine alone, plummet down and down, down until, finally, I slide into a further darkness which becomes sleep. Amidst scattered dreams I hear a song about a lion sleeping tonight. I'm smiling as I listen. Or maybe I'm on the verge of tears.

Storm Damage

The weatherman, his voice monotone as ever, warned of a freak storm on the way. Lightning and torrential rain, hurricane-force winds.

Jack McGill rocked his head. 'I knew it, I knew it,' he said. He swallowed the last of his tea, rose, crossed to the old Pilot radio and silenced it. 'Come on.'

'Go ahead,' said Timmy. 'I'll be straight after.'

'What's holding you?'

'Spot, what about Spot? Do you not think he has a mouth too?'

'Don't heed the dog, he won't starve. You heard what the wireless said.'

'Go down, go down. Talking won't save hay.'

Jack shuffled out, grumbling, into the humidity of the August morning. All traces of earlier fog were burned clean from the domes of the local hills, all nine cairns vividly silhouetted against a sky of innocent blue – breast-like, nipples of stone. It was scorching. Barely gone eight o'clock but feeling more like mid-afternoon. Too hot. A bad sign.

The brothers worked with a vigour and efficiency belying their years; they worked in silence. Jack gathered in and raked while Timmy did the building and plucking. The cocks rose at an encouraging rate, each an exact replica of the one before.

Spot lay in the token shade of a lone willow, flat as if shotgunned.

By noon, the larger of the two bottoms was secured. A dozen sturdy cocks headed and combed and triple-roped.

'G'over and get the water. We'll take a breather.'

'Sound.'

Timmy headed across to the drain and fished the gallon from its cool bed of mud. Spot rose from the dead and shambled back after him.

The coned shadow of that twelfth cock clouded with smoke as the McGills, scented hay cushioning their backs, puffed in unison their Briar pipes, fingers hooked round warm bowls. Soon, though, they were talking big wind. Debbie was recalled, the worst blow of all. The end of September '61, the country ripped asunder. Over thirty years had passed but time couldn't dim the memory of Debbie.

'Come on,' cried Jack suddenly and they rose as one to attack the little triangular bottom. They were hungry but it was no day for the belly.

The sky was stainless by the time the last cock was secured, the valley a bowl of concentrated heat and hush. Both men leant on their toil.

'Maybe we should throw another oul' rope on them,' mused Jack presently.

They did so.

It was agreeably cool in the cottage kitchen, its small window and porched doorway admitting little sun.

Spot sat watch on the stone threshold, sniffing the outer air.

'Look at himself with his smelling,' said Jack. 'She won't be long now.'

'I see him,' said Timmy.

'A sight, that. Dogs can deck a storm ten mile off, maybe further.'

'So they say, so they say.'

'The goat's hair, I never seen it wrong yet. Never. That sky yesterday, 'twas fleeced with it.'

'They were often wrong, as often wrong as right,' said Timmy, as he upped from the table and made for his armchair, one of two either side of the dead hearth. Jack followed suit. They got out their pipes. What was coming would come; it wasn't right to be talking about such things.

Inside an hour they'd dozed off. Spot kept lone watch.

They stirred awake as the clock struck its first of six gongs; they eyed each other sheepishly and then looked to the door. All was still, a canvas of sun imprinted on the floor of the porch. Better g'out and take a look, Jack thought. As he came back in he was talking to himself.

They resumed their wait, hunched and rigid now, staring into the ashes. No fire would be put down until the blast had come and gone. The chimney might take light, burn them from house and home. Wind was deadly.

'I don't like it,' said Jack, and he rose and moped towards the door.

Just gone half seven the eastern horizon started to darken. With this change came a dramatic cooling of the air and soon the first whispers of wind trembled the tips of the fir trees at the end of the haggard.

The McGills stood on their doorstep. Thunder rumbled, somewhere up beyond Boyle, and gradually deepened its tone. They retreated inside, shut the door, shot its sturdy bolt.

The wind blew like a natural wind at first but quickly it noised towards a wilder element. The cottage kitchen gloomed, the roof iron began to screech, the men prayed. A bucket clanged over the stony street until it became airborne and noised no more. Thunder rumbled ever louder, and sporadic forks of lightning flash-lit the tableau of the McGills within.

And then, at last, came the rain – sudden and torrential. Flooding down onto the roof, bringing calm to man and beast beneath. The worst was over.

Jack rose and placed his beads back on the horsenail. 'I'll take a peep out, see what it's doing.'

The rich smells of the earth seeped into the cottage, and abroad all was well again with the world. Every fir in the shelter belt standing tall and familiar; the rain-darkened cocks squatting safe in the bottoms.

'Thanks be to the Lord,' said Timmy as he joined Jack in the doorway.

'Amen.'

They fell silent for several minutes, as if awed by the utter stillness. The low sky steadily unloaded itself and a veritable river washed down the street. Gradually, birds in thorny bushes resumed their calling to song.

'I fear she passed over too quick,' mused Jack, his tone slowed and wary under the burden of his conviction. 'There's another blast left in her.'

'Do you think?'

'I'm telling you. She'll be back with a vengeance …'

'God forbid.'

'Aye. All we can do I suppose is –'

'Sshh!' hushed Timmy, pointing away down the street.

'What? What's up with you?'

'Below in the hayshed.'

Jack looked.

'Leaning up ag'inst the horsecart. Do you not see him?'

'I do. It's not Doherty, is it?'

'Cripes, man. Wher'd he appear out of?'

'Damned if I know.'

'Shout at him. Give him a shout.'

'Steady.'

'Go on. Sure he could be drownded, the poor *gasún.*'

Jack hesitated, curiosity vying with ingrained caution. He adjusted his cap. 'Hello!' he ventured finally.

The figure in the hayshed turned sharply and, after a moment, waved and said: 'Hi! Hi there!'

'Jaze it's a woman … a young lassie,' said Timmy, urgently nudging Jack.

'Can I come on up?' she called, already starting forward, a small bag or some such possession held atop her head as she braved the deluge.

By now Spot, his route of attack blocked by his masters in the doorway, had broken into a croaky fit of barking.

'Go in and hold the dog,' said Jack. 'Do ya hear me, stop gawking and go in.' Timmy muttered privately as he wheeled inside.

The stranger delivered a toothpaste smile to the door. 'Some day, huh.'

'Come in, come in.' Jack gestured her in. 'You're – you're drownded.'

She ducked through and offered a 'Hi' to Timmy, who appeared to be in the process of strangling the silenced Spot. He nodded, that and no more.

Another limp-arm gesture from Jack, an arc of unsureness: 'Sit down.'

She sat. Water trickled from her boots and wormed along the flag floor.

She maintained her smile, acutely aware of the men's shyness, attempting to put them at their ease.

A long half minute passed, the McGills cast adrift in their own house.

'I was up on the hills,' she explained then, the bloated silence having made her feel vaguely on trial. 'Exploring the cairns and stuff. Sheltered in your shed ...' She quietly inflated her lungs; her palms slid along her denimed thighs as if ironing them. 'That storm, it just ... happened.'

'The mountain,' muttered Jack with a degree of relief. He looked over at his brother and nodded. 'She was on the mountain.'

'I heard, I heard,' said Timmy.

'It's really something up there,' she said.

'I know what you mean,' said Jack. He gaped blankly about the kitchen for a few moments and then pulled up a chair from beside the dresser. Timmy, his head bowed, kept Spot pinned between his low palms.

'Will that rain never stop? I gotta be getting back soon.'

'And where would that be now? – if you don't mind me asking.'

'Sligo. Hitchhiked from there this afternoon.'

'Sligo. That was a queer journey.'

'I got a straight ride. Nice lady, drew me a map to the cairns an' all.'

'You're staying there, like?' ventured Jack, bolder now as he started to cut at the tobacco. 'Touring about?' He scribed a large circle in the air with his penknife.

'Just passing through. I'll stay for one more day, maybe.'

Jack, his pipe fired, forged on. 'You'd be from America, I'd be saying.'

The visitor smiled wryly. 'Yeah, I guess you can hear that.'

'I can. There's no mistaking the Yankee tongue.' He spat into the ashes and turned to Timmy: no response. *Won't open his mouth. Sitting there like a dummy.*

'By the way, I'm Kathleen.' She bounced out of her chair and speared out a confident hand to the McGills, Jack first.

'Jack McGill,' said Jack. 'And that's Timmy,' he was forced to add when the latter offered his hand but refused to part with his name.

'Jack and Timmy. It sure is good to meet you guys.'

Jack savoured a few steady puffs, the rhythmic smack of his lips slower than the clock but just as regular. 'Kathleen. A grand name, that. Irish.'

'Yeah, my mom's folks came from County Wexford. I gotta make a trip down there before I head back home.'

Jack turned to Timmy. 'Take a look out and see what it's doing.'

Timmy rose sharply. Spot padded over to Kathleen and sniffed at her boots. She patted him and talked doggie talk.

'Well?'

'Still coming down in buckets.'

'Any stir of a breeze?'

'No.' Timmy stayed rooted to the step until finally Jack angled his head and said: 'Come in, come in, you won't improve it by looking at it. And throw on the kettle!'

'No-no, I'm fine,' said Kathleen. 'Don't wanna put you to any trouble.'

But already Timmy was making for the cooker, happy to hide in a chore.

'This is quite a place you got here,' she remarked presently. She stood and stretched herself into an X of ease. 'First time I've actually been in one of these cottages.'

'It's all right, I suppose,' said Jack. 'It's a roof.'

As the kettle started to sing Timmy flipped the hinged lid of the teapot to gain his brother's attention. 'Do you want some?'

'Aye, aye, we'll have a drop. And take out that brack and cut it up. Not too thick.'

Kathleen went to the door. 'So much rain,' she mused aloud, stabbing her hands into the back pockets of her jeans as she gazed across the valley.

The tea was a rough-and-ready affair but Kathleen, her appetite honed by her airy climb, wolfed down the slabs of brack and drank, with relish, the strong brew. Her hand brushed Timmy's as they reached simultaneously to claim more brack, the latter's sharply withdrawing.

'Go on, can't you leave the rest of that for the visitor,' checked Jack, giving his brother a withering stare. 'And make more tea. Sure you didn't wet half enough.'

After nine the rain ceased as abruptly as it had begun and a weak light filtered into the kitchen. Kathleen strode out to the street and looked at the murky sky and the shrouds of mist veiling the heathery slopes.

Jack came as far as the doorway and he, too, surveyed the local world.

'Seems like it's over at last,' Kathleen said. 'Guess I'd better make tracks if I'm gonna get to Sligo before nightfall.'

He gazed at her, his eyes dull marbles of unease, and then he gazed again towards the signposts of weather. 'I wouldn't be venturing far yet, girl,' he advised in a sombre tone. 'There's more to come, I fear.'

'Yeah, well, I get wet I get wet,' she said. 'I can make it down to the highway in twenty minutes. One good ride then and I'm in Sligo.'

She turned to go back in for her hiking pack.

'Com'ere, just take a look yonder,' said Jack, pointing the shank of his pipe towards the nebulous hills. 'You see that?'

Kathleen looked and when she saw nothing untoward she shrugged.

'Yon bullocks of Doherty's. Lookit the way they're all bunched together. Feared. Take my advice, girl, and stay where y'are.'

She sighed dramatically. 'But I gotta get to Sligo. I have plans, I've arranged to meet somebody.'

'I know about plans, I know all about plans, but I'm thinking you'll see no Sligo this night. Look now! What did I tell ya!'

Kathleen followed the arrow of the shank.

'Lightning,' said Jack, and as he uttered the word another faint flash zigzagged from the gunmetal horizon. 'Come in, girl, come in and sit down. You don't understand the thing like I do,' he said, turning on his heel.

The second wind laid siege to the cottage within two minutes of the door being bolted. This time, there was no lightning to flash the interior, and if thunder neared it wasn't audible; this time, there was nothing save the howled essence of the blast itself.

A hurricane which the weatherman, come tomorrow, would call by the name Charlie.

The McGills prayed without the guide of their beads but soon, as the storm crashed again and again against the door, as moments of ominous lull gave way to gusts of renewed ferocity, Jack was reaching towards the horsenail and the words of the rosary were given full and urgent voice.

Our Father, who art in Heaven, hallowed be thy name ...

The kitchen grew ever darker, due as much to the hour as the hurricane, and Kathleen was grateful for this cover. It shaded her agnostic eye.

Hail Mary, full of grace, the Lord is with thee ...

As she listened to the murmured chorus of the McGills, a line she'd once read somewhere stole into her mind: Those who come to mock remain to pray. The line took on new life now, here in the near dark in this cottage in the west of Ireland. Her gaze wandered from the pair of shadow figures by the hearth and settled on the glow of the bulb before the Sacred Heart picture. For a few moments, she slipped beyond the reach of intellect into a state of non-thought, a zone hushed with wonder.

Spot came to her, whimpering, and nestled his head in the refuge of her crotch. She caressed him; the panic in his animal heart entered her palms.

Abroad, the wind still howled in its elemental rage, noising through the tunnel of her inner ear. She might have been adrift on the open sea.

She found herself transported back up to the high ground. Imagining what it must feel like to be alone there now, utterly alone in the lee of a cairn.

Holy Mary, mother of God, pray for us sinners…

'It's over … gone,' said Jack, his tone still solemn, locked in the key of prayer. The springs of the chair creaked in the silence as he adjusted his stiff pose. 'Thanks be to the good Lord.' When Timmy didn't respond he suddenly remembered there was a third person sitting in the shadows. 'The light, the light,' he muttered. 'Get up and switch on the light.'

Timmy's tack boots rasped on stone. Power could be out, he thought, and a part of him wished it so, wished for the night's continued cloak.

Spot flopped from Kathleen's lap, his tail fanning vigorously as a bulb lit the kitchen and his masters. Jack turned to Kathleen. He wanted to say something casual, maybe even jokey, but instead found himself restricted to a self-conscious nod. Me pipe, he thought. He lifted it from the hob, arcing an eye onto Timmy as he did so. No aid from that quarter. He bit on the shank, plundered his

pocket of the tobacco. He again turned to Kathleen. 'We were saying a few prayers there ...' he said, his body language a hybrid of
unease and apology. He raked a splayed hand along his jaws. 'I'm
glad you took my advice, girl,' he continued. 'If you were out in that,
God only knows what'd happen.' He smiled, or tried to.

Kathleen's returned smile was freer. 'I'm glad, too,' she said.

The glare of the unshaded bulb exposed the McGills like a stage
spotlight.

'I wonder how are our cocks, Timmy? Any of them standing at
all?'

Kathleen bit her lip.

'We'll not know till morning, I suppose', said Timmy. 'Can't stir
out now.'

Good boy yourself, thought Jack, heartened by the easiness of
the reply.

Kathleen pondered hard. She checked her watch again: 10.14.
The music session in Sligo would soon be starting. She thought of
the serpentine lane that took her into the valley, and how it would
be hidden in darkness. No, she decided quickly. I'll crash here for
the night ... that's if they ...?

Silence. Say something, she told herself. Keep talking. 'I guess
you get a load of those storms here in Ireland. With the ocean and
all that,' she struggled to clarify, her hands gesturing without any
focus.

'No, not so much. Seldom you see one bad as tonight. That was
a right boyo. Dangerous. Deadly dangerous.'

'Mmm.' She rose, absently pursing her lips, and crossed to the
darkened window. The men watched her, read her thoughts. She
saw her reflection in the glass and, for a moment, it spooked her. She
turned to the McGills. Her eyes alone asked the required question.

Jack spat into the hearth and then, with almost theatrical delib-
eration, got to his feet. 'Girl, there's a roof here,' he said, 'and you're

welcome to stay under it. More than welcome. Isn't that right, Timmy?'

' 'Tis.' Timmy's eye met Kathleen's; his face thawed into a smile and she felt relief on seeing this.

'Right, that's settled,' chirped Jack. 'And now that we've a visitor for the night,' he added buoyantly, 'I think we ought to put down a spark.'

Timmy upped and tipped fuel from the full jute bag.

Ash crackled and spat and brown turf flamed moodily and Jack McGill's mind slipped all storm shadows as he delighted in the warmth of a young voice. The company, so long since they'd had a bit of company. More tea was made, eggs boiled, the last of the brack polished off. The job was oxo.

Kathleen, for her part, was on cloud nine. Nowhere in the pages of her trusty guidebook was there a signpost to such hidden wonders. Trad sessions could wait; tonight belonged to lore.

She asked about the cairns and Jack told her all he knew, which wasn't a lot. 'Musha, they were always there, just as ya seen them. Comical yokes.' The same man, though, had other and livelier landscapes to paint. Stories passed down from his father, passed down from a long line of McGills.

Cormac McAirt suckled by a she-wolf in the coves of Keash. 'The Devil's Bit': 'Yon gap in the mountain – the Divil himself chewed a lump out of it as he flew across.' The doing-in of Danny Meehan: 'Battered to death with a loy, and all over a disputed right of way.' The Red Muldowney: 'He'd the strength of three men, lifted Kerr's ass clean off the hoof and the world watching. Me father, God be good to him, could tell ya, Kathleen. He seen it done.' The Dead Lake over Dooagh direction: 'The Mallon lads defied the curse and paid dearly.' Mad O'Rourke, the go-the-road, feared for the evil eye. The fairy fort, where Doherty's mother saw the little people burying one of their own: 'Thousands of them, all in a twisty line!'

On and on the stories meandered, the valley and its gone people bustling afresh with life – ghosts returned to reclaim their plots of foamy ground.

Kathleen, her eyes aglow, fuelled by a mixture of fascination and amusement, never tired of listening. And never did she forget to hold a door of her mind ajar for Timmy, willing him to come in from the cold.

For Timmy – hunched, staring into the fire, attentive only to his pipe – cut a lonely figure indeed. Not a word out of him. His thoughts sombre and deep as the coves facing Keash, his thoughts webbed by a woman from Keash.

Not for maybe forty years had Maura McPadden returned with such clarity to his mind. Walking across the hills with a flashlamp to meet her; floating home in the dawn, his head light with possibility. Twenty-two she was then, nimble as a deer. Boston, she was mad for Boston. An aunt there, plenty of quick money. Wanted Timmy to go with her. They'd save up, they'd get married. But Timmy hesitated too long and lost her.

She wrote for him; she told him of wonders. No, he wouldn't budge. In time, he heard she'd taken another. Bob Maye from Threenbeg. The size of Boston and she ended up meeting and marrying a man born not two crow's miles from her home door. That hit Timmy hard. Losing her he'd almost come to terms with but losing her to a one-time neighbour kept the sore open. Never being one for the bottle, he threw himself into slave work instead. Breaking rocks for Council roads at five bob a week, digging trenches deep enough to swallow a cow. The stain of regret eventually left him but there was nothing of value to take its place. Just a daily tide of days without dream of difference, unending. He never courted again.

He stirred in his chair and sighed heavily, saw his pipe had gone out. Jack heard his sigh and read it as a sign to shut up. 'Kathleen, *a grá*, I'm hoarse talking,' he concluded. 'Like a windmill when I get going.'

'A windmill is the word,' said Timmy, brightening. He cupped a match to his pipe, puffed it back to life and winked at Kathleen through the smoke.

Kathleen grabbed her chance. 'I got something here to show you.' Up she sprang, grinning promisingly as she fished the pack of photographs from a side pocket of her hiking bag. Polaroid snapshots of the cairns – feelers towards the more studious images hidden away in her 35mm. The mens' faces lit up with anticipation. She halved the pack and brought drama to bear as she handed them over.

Silence. Shoulders squirming, eyes scanning, smiles bright as the fire. 'Begod that's them surely,' Jack announced presently. 'Clear as day.' He turned to his brother. 'Gimme a squint at your ones.' They swapped.

Kathleen watched them, Timmy especially: so good to see him engaged. Now was the moment. 'How about a shot of yourselves?' Her tone was suitably heady, as if the idea had only then occurred to her. 'Got a flash an' all … right here in my bag.'

The McGills stared at her, and then at each other; their slowly emerging grins linked them, engendered trust. Timmy nodded, a chin-dip saying yes.

She uncased $850 worth of Hasselblad and told them to get ready.

'Just wanna shoot one with this … for myself.' The men stood; she stood. 'Wait,' cried Jack. 'Hold on there a minute, stall the diggers.' He got his Sunday cap, Timmy's too. 'Better with these boys on us.'

Kathleen couldn't stop smiling. 'There? What about there by the window?'

'Sound,' said Jack. 'Come on, Timmy. Are we all right now like this?'

She gazed all round the kitchen, tugged reflectively at her nose. 'Let's try here instead,' she said, steering them across to the dresser. A smoke-browned statue of Christ, arms outstretched, stood tall on top of it.

'You want to take th'oul dresser too?'

'Uh-huh.' She hunkered, fitted all in. 'Okay, stay real steady.'

'Hold on! Wait! Tell us when you're ready.'

'I'm ready. Stand a bit closer. Thaaat's it … Okay!'

'You have us?' blinked Jack.

'Stay there, don't move. One more … beautiful!'

As she put the Hasselblad back into its case, the McGills thawed free of their pose and looked at each other, wondering where the pictures were. But then they saw the Polaroid Instamatic emerging from the bag and they decided to trust that.

'Okay, guys, get yourselves ready again. Maybe try over by the fire this time.' They went to the fire, obedient as collies, and stood close.

Kathleen talked them to ease, then hit the button. Within seconds, the square of Polaroid paper had been ejected. 'Stay there, don't move.' She clicked her fingers as she waited impatiently for the image to find definition and when it did she nodded her satisfaction. 'Now, okay, last one … Gotcha!'

'One apiece,' said Jack to Timmy, beside himself with excitement.

Less than a minute later the brothers were making for their chairs, each in possession of a clean snap, their grins broad as May dawn. As they sat, the same thought occurred to both and they looked to the corner where Spot lay sprawled in dead sleep. She should have took him, too. A pity. Aye.

They studied themselves as they'd studied the druids' cairns; clean caps were adjusted, lips pursed, the little squares handled with precious care.

'Mighty yokes, cameras,' mused Jack. 'Us to a T.' They exchanged snaps, engaged in further study.

Timmy it was who gave the ultimate seal of approval. 'Wait'll the bucko sees these,' he muttered proudly. 'The bucko' was Freddie Doherty, eighty years old and half blind, the valley's only other survivor.

The night took a dip after the thrill of being photographed had exhausted itself. The three were like family going through the motions of small talk, in the knowledge that the clock is ticking down to the moment for partings – a hackney car due, a son or daughter heading off to faraway places.

The grandfather clock struck one. Timmy eyed it, eyed his brother. 'Aye, I suppose we'd better be making a shape for the bunk,' said Jack. He slapped his thighs and nodded awkwardly at Kathleen.

'Hope I didn't keep you up,' she said, wincing slightly.

Timmy stood. Self-consciousness caused his gaze to wander all round the kitchen before finally landing on Kathleen. 'I'll be saying goodbye to you now, Kathleen – in case you're away up the lane when we rise. And may God mind you,' he tailed off, his eyes dipping. She rose, thinking to give him a hug or a peck on the cheek. Too late. Timmy was already sloping towards the lower room, his shoulders drooped, fingers scraping at his temple.

Kathleen resumed her seat, figuring it was Jack's privilege to snap the cord of the night in his own time. Maybe he had more to say.

No, he had no more to say. He got to his feet. Then, fingering his jowl, he considered, for the first time, where the visitor might actually sleep. Flustered, muttering as he went, he headed down to consult with Timmy.

Kathleen listened to the low urgency of voices breaking from the bedroom and quickly she came to understand the problem. I can crash in this chair, she thought. Poor guys … She rose and paced the flagged floor, eyeing the religious effigies, the dreaming dog, the Polaroid snaps proud against the breast of the ancient radio.

'Do you think,' said Jack, emerging from the bedroom, 'would you be all right in one of them oul' chairs? You can put on more fire and I'll get a coat or something to throw over you.'

'Of course.' She went to him, squeezed his arm. 'The chair's perfect.'

'It's just … the upper room's a sight, full of trumpery.'

'It's okay, Jack, I understand. The chair's fine. Really.'

'Are you sure now?'

'Sure I'm sure.'

'Sound. Wait'll I see so about the coat.'

'Jack, please,' said Kathleen. 'I don't need any coat or anything.' She squeezed his arm again, the gesture pure instinct. 'Come on, time for your beauty sleep,' she chirped, struggling for gaiety, some small lift for an old man's mood. She took Jack McGill's hand and sandwiched her palms about it for a moment before easing him towards the lower room. 'Take care … both of you,' she said. 'I'll treasure this night.' Jack nodded, unable to find the right words, or any words at all. His eyes, alone, spoke. The door creaked open onto blanket dark, creaked slowly shut.

*

Timmy, his sleep having been troubled by ragged dreams, woke early. Light flooded the room. Outside, birds warbled on branch and wire, thrilled in their instinct. Habitually, he looked to the chair by the bed: no clock.

Then his mind slipped its shadow and he remembered …

He pushed onto his elbow, cocked an anxious ear towards the kitchen. The silence and his held breath became one. He stifled a yawn, lay back down.

The grandfather clock ticked ever closer to eight. Timmy could hear its ticks. He stiffened as the first gong rang out, stayed stiff as he counted seven further gongs. *Eight o'clock ... wonder is she gone?* Jack still snored by his side; Timmy thought to rouse him but, lured by some latent and acutely private want, resisted the urge. He listened. The birds continued to warble; the clock ticked, a heartbeat in his head. Above and beyond these sounds, the valley's enormous hush remained constant.

Only when the dog finally shambled to the door, raised a paw and scraped at it, did his master feel free to emerge from hiding.

The kitchen was as always, everything in its frozen place; no sign at all that a woman had spent the night there. Timmy stood rooted, staring at the chair Kathleen had made her own. Spot whimpered for attention and he aimed a kick at him. He thought of the photos and turned to the radio. There was now a note there too. He read, read it again, folded it carefully and slid it into his pocket. Got his cap and headed off out. Spot didn't follow.

Jack rose fifteen minutes later. He didn't even think to check the time, the photos claiming his first and full attention. His shoulders jigged as he eyed them. One grand lassie, he thought, smiling. Never in me life seen friendlier. And then he thought: *Where's himself?*

He wasn't in the bottoms. A few of the cocks seemed in bad shape but no trace of Timmy. He tried the cowhouse: no cow in yet. Maybe he was gone to check the sheep? ... but he always brought the dog ... *That's comical.*

Jack hastened to the sandy knoll near the manure heap and scanned all around. He raised his hand against the sun's dazzle; Spot stood by his side, ears cocked, tail motionless.

'There he is, Spot! What in the name a Christ took him ...?'

Timmy was over in the hill field, standing close to the lone blackthorn. Keash mountain behind him, blue sky above. He appeared bent as the bush.

A good five minutes passed, neither man moving.

'I have it,' mused Jack aloud. He rocked his head, the action suggestive of a wise elder sadly, noting the young losing their way.

Only from that high ground where Timmy stood could he follow the whole loop of the lane, track it and anyone on it right up to the pinnacle where it dipped sharply away towards the main road. Jack now watched through his brother's stilled eye, saw the departing girl climbing, climbing, until she was silhouetted against the sky.

Back inside, Jack sat heavily. He got his pipe but his mind wandered away from lighting it. He eyed the clock and it said it was time to be warming up the wireless for the news but he didn't do that either. A strange quiet closed in on him: the quiet of an empty kitchen, the quiet of a brother.

He was again lost in the photos when he heard Timmy's boots grate on the cottage step. Shiftily, he replaced them and turned on the wireless, then turned away to busy himself at the gas cooker. 'It's well time for the bit of breakfast, I suppose,' he said, and as he spoke he was acutely aware of the strained note in his voice. Yet he had to keep talking. 'There's a big baulk of an ash blocking the lane – we'll have to get the crosscut at it. And the cocks are badly tattered.' He flashed a jug of water into the kettle. 'And God only knows what more damage is done.'

'Aye, that's it,' sighed Timmy, stooping to pat Spot as the Pilot radio warmed finally towards voice, bringing distant news of who could say what.

Inklings of Sin

I'm squashing my face deep into the pillow so Tim won't hear me crying. He's wide awake. I can feel it: his stiffness, the way he has curled himself into a ball. I'm a ball too. My knees are nearly touching my chin.

They are still gabbing down in the parlour, the whole gang of them. Such a buzz. Drinking away like mad, you can be sure. Crates of every sort piled in the porch. Porter and whiskey and beer. And sherry for the women.

I squeeze the pillow as another loud laugh shivers up through the ceiling. Tim stirs a bit, and I can hear him swallowing. He's going over – same as me. I just know he is. I want to turn the light on, force him to talk, but I can't let him see me blubbering like this. I'm ten, I'm not a child anymore.

What got me all sad was the sight of Granny's face. It seemed to appear out of the dark as soon as Tim turned off the light and crept in beside me. She was smiling, same as always. Happy as Larry.

The thought of her down in that grave was bad enough, but then my head filled with crawly pictures and that's when I started crying. The thing is I think they killed her, them below in the kitchen. Not smashed her with a hammer or something, but forced her to die all the same. Rushed her.

Last week, that's when the whole trouble started. Saturday. Myself and Tim were over in Granny's house, just like every other Saturday. Fooling around, having a great time. Climbing the trees behind the henhouse, walking on the tricky wall of the tank, rooting through hundreds of old bottles out the back. Stuff like that.

Course, we had to do all the jobs first. Bringing in the turf and emptying the ashes from the buckets and dumping the junk she'd piled in boxes during the week. We always did them jobs, me and Tim, ever since I was tiny. Mammy told us to because, I suppose, Granny being her mother, she wanted her given a hand. Or maybe she just wanted us out of her sight for a while. A bit of both, I'd say. Grown-ups are sly that way.

Anyway, it suited us down to the ground. Saturday's the worst possible day at home. Big brothers hanging round, watching stupid racing and stuff on the television. Even Daddy, and he's not too mad on sport. The grunty wrestlers he watches, of all things. The chair beside the screen and him puffing away like a chimney. If you made one sound when they were on you'd be in the soup. No, we were better off in Granny's. We could do as we liked there.

I don't know why but I'd a feeling something was wrong when I spotted Uncle Frank landing on Granny's street. He's not seen around much because he lives far away. Near Dublin, I think. Christmas is the most time you see him – and even then only a few hours or so. He has a huge car, faster-looking than any of the ones at Mass. A hundred and thirty on the clock. It'd do it too, I reckon, or damn near. Tim thinks so anyway. It's a brute, he always says, a fecking brute. He gave us a spin in it once, Uncle Frank. Just down to the cross and back, but even in that distance you'd know it was speedy. The lovely sound of the engine, smooth as a cat purring after a feed.

Well, he can stuff his bloody car! I'm not sitting in it again, that's for certain. Him and his fat cigars. He's the one I blame most.

Jesus, listen to them ... couldn't care less. Killers, that's what the lot of youse are. Killers!

Me and Tim were a good way up the dangerous sycamore, checking all round us, holding on with one hand, when the black car slowed to a halt on the gravel. It's Uncle Frank, it's Uncle Frank, Tim yapped, and off down with him like a squirrel. He jumped from the second-last branch, landed on the skiddy leaves and ended up on his arse. I loved that, I really loved that. Come on, he called, come on down quick and we can sit in her. I took it nice and steady, branch after branch, pretending I didn't care about the brute. My arse stayed dry.

There was a butt of a cigar in the ashtray and Tim dived straight for it. Then he started into the pulling and puffing – as if it were lit, acting all important, the very same as Uncle Frank. I pressed the radio buttons but got no music or nothing. He brought the keys in with him, stupid, says Tim. And he left his cigar lit, did he? says I back, real cool. That shut him up.

We tried every lever and button and knob but the only thing we got to work was the small light in the roof. And a lot of good that was. Tim grabbed the steering wheel then, like he was driving. Even started making car noises and talking in a funny voice: Fifty, sixty, seventy, eighty, ninety, a hundred, ZZZ!! – hold on tight, we're coming to a bad bend – EEE!!!! He swung on the wheel until there was a hard click and it locked, wouldn't turn any more. He looked crookedly over at me, terrified. Now, who's that stupid? I said, but I was terrified too. We kept trying the wheel – it was no use, we couldn't get it to turn. Tim's hands were shaking and he was gone white as a ghost.

Hop out, hop out quick! he said finally, and we were off like hares.

We hid round by the gable and the first thing Tim did was take out his thing and piss. He didn't aim high, though, like we do in the game – his shoes got sprayed a bit. I passed no heed. Listen, he said, we'll head into the house, pretending we didn't see the car, and then act real surprised.

Why can't we just go home? I said.

He thought about this for a minute and tugged at his nose. No, that'd make it worse, he said. Just do as I do, right?

I nodded and followed him. A snail could nearly have caught up with us.

The shock of seeing who was in Granny's kitchen made me forget all about the wheel.

Uncle Frank I was ready for but, Jesus, Uncle Liam was there as well – however he managed to sneak in without us spotting him. The pair of them, tall as soldiers, planted in the middle of the floor.

Tim must have got a shock too because he forgot to act surprised.

They stopped talking as we walked in. Just stopped dead and gawked at us. Something was going on, for sure. I'd seen other grown-ups with the same look a few times – and it always meant trouble of some sort.

Well, if it's not the hard men themselves, Uncle Frank said then, reaching a hand out to ruffle our heads. I hated that, having my hair messed.

Listen, childer, run back home quick or your father'll be worried. Mammy's voice, Mammy was there too! I looked at her. She was over in the corner, her chair pulled close to Granny's chair, chewing her top lip and fiddling with the buttons of her cardigan. I stopped looking at her.

Go on, kids, do as your mother says, said Uncle Frank. My eyes had dropped to the floor now but I could feel his dark shadow and smell his fresh cigar.

I turned away to the door, shoving Tim ahead of me; then we both flew.

Did you hear what he called us? says Tim, once we were back in the safe spot by the gable – Kids! He was pissing again, and grinning, the broken steering wheel gone clean out of his mind. I wasn't thinking of it either. Not then.

What's up? says he, jerking his zip shut and looking at me funny.

Nothing, says I, nothing wrong with me.

No, I mean in there, he says. They're planning something.

After a few minutes we, too, started planning, then shot off quietly.

I was glad I had my grippy shoes on as we edged along the inside wall of the tank, coming from opposite ends so both of us could get close to the kitchen window. Sitting down was tricky, but we managed it. Once we were settled, our legs dangling above the water, we cocked our ears and began to listen hard.

The window was open a few inches in the bottom, an old polish tin holding it up. Uncle Frank was spouting away, as usual. I thought I smelt his cigar smoke stinking out to us, but maybe I imagined that part. Uncle Liam mumbled something then, and a long silence followed. Not one sound, you'd think they were struck dumb in there.

All of a sudden, I could make out someone crying and knew straight away it was Mammy. I looked at Tim. He was like a statue, his eyes lost in the tank.

I got afraid. Grown-ups don't cry for nothing.

There was more talk, stopping and starting, but most of it was fierce low. Like they were half afraid someone might be about, listening to their plans.

The walls have ears, I often heard Granny saying.

I twisted round on the tank till I was flat on my belly and held on tight. Then I chanced an eye in by the side of the polish box. Tim just kept biting his nails and staring down into the dark water.

Granny was in her big armchair by the fire, same as always. Our two uncles were sitting now, legs crossed and swinging. Mammy had stood up. She wasn't fiddling with her buttons any more; her arms were wrapped tight, like she was hugging herself: her head was down and I got the feeling she wasn't one bit happy.

Over the next ten minutes or so I heard the whole thing, although I didn't know rightly what it meant. Granny was going to a new house. The something Home, it was called, and Uncle Frank kept on saying how lovely a place it was. 'Excellent,' he said. And 'Fantastic'. Big words like that. I think it started with T, or W. 'Twas a wild odd name. Foreign maybe.

Granny seemed lost, her wiry hands wriggling as if she were at her beads.

Mammy suddenly started bawling again and Uncle Frank said Shh and then he scratched his head, said that it had to be done, it was for the best. Jesus, I thought, the man was raving. I wished Granny would say her bit, put him in his box. Getting packed off to a strange house at her age? And if it was far away how would me and Tim visit her and do the jobs for her? None of it made an ounce of sense. She was happy where she was – any fool could see that.

I wanted to run home and get Daddy. I reached to Tim, pinched his leg; he wouldn't look at me.

Then things started to speed up. Uncle Frank said something to Uncle Liam – right into his ear – before turning to Mammy, touching her on the arm. Nodding, he chucked his cigar butt into the coals and headed for the door.

I nearly toppled into the tank as I straightened up, forgetting I was on a narrow wall. Come on! said Tim, already jumping down and flying away through the apple trees, keeping low.

We were both panting as we peeped out from the corner of the hen-house to see what Uncle Frank was up to. He got a big blue case from the boot of the car, stared hard at it for several seconds, as if thinking it might bite him, and then banged the boot shut. The day seemed to turn fierce quiet and icy as he headed back into the house. I could hear his bunch of keys tinkling, and the click of his shoes on the path. The birds kept at it in the whitethorns but their singing didn't sound normal. Too bare or something. Whistly. Nearly as if they knew there was trouble. And maybe they did? Birds are no joke.

I looked at Tim and he looked at me but neither of us said a word. Neither of us made a move either; just stood there like zombies, afraid to go round to the tank again, afraid of what we might see.

Why? I kept asking myself, as I remembered all the stuff I'd heard through the window. The more I thought about it, the more awful I felt. And then it dawned on me that Granny probably knew nothing about going into this new home. She was stone deaf, and none of them shouted anything into her ear. Not when I was peeping in anyway. The whole thing was daft, pure madness.

I said a bit of a prayer but doubted it would do any good. It was too late.

Poor mother is a bother now and needs full-time care, Uncle Frank had said. His voice rushed back into my head, spouting that horrible line over and over again. I scratched a sharp stone into the plaster of the henhouse and cursed under my breath. I was trying to figure out what 'full-time care' really meant when, just then, the

door opened. Tim clawed my shoulder. Look, he said, they're bringing Granny. He clawed harder, his nails dug into me, but I said nothing. Our heads came close, touched. We kept watching, watching.

Uncle Frank and Uncle Liam were steering Granny slowly along
the path. She looked tiny between them – nearly like a child. She
doesn't want to go, I started to say, but Tim clapped a quick hand
across my mouth and held it there.

Mammy appeared then, the big blue case hanging from her arm.
She walked as slow as the others, if not slower, like she was in a
trance or something. We could hear her sniffling.

Granny's head twisted around as they lifted her into the car.
Maybe to get a last look at the house? I went cold all over, a real
strange feeling.

Mammy squeezed in beside her and Uncle Frank closed the door.

The wheel! said Tim. Oh shit!! It dawned on me after a second
but I didn't care. Granny was all I could think of, that picture of
them carrying her out the path, forcing her to go. The two front
doors banged shut, the car ticked over for awhile, and then off they
went to God knows where.

The damn wheel wasn't broken at all. I wish it was! I wish he'd
driven his big car into the quarry and split his stupid head! Poor
Granny …

They're still at it below.

I'm trying to imagine what sort of place it was, that new home they
pushed Granny into. A nursing home, Mammy called it, but you
can't heed everything she says. She's nearly as bad as the rest of
them. You can go visit her in a few weeks, she said. A few weeks!
They dumped her, as far as I can see. What else could you call it?
Got her out of the way, just because she was getting a bit doddery on
the legs. Why couldn't we mind her at home? Even bring her over
here? Nurses, I know what they are. Nice women who wear white

and are deadly for looking after people. But they're still strangers. Granny'd have hated them, I'm certain she would. They'd be at her to do stuff. Making her wear new clothes, maybe, or taking away her heavy boots and hiding them. And then all the praying she used to do, I wouldn't be surprised if they nabbed her beads and relics. Must have been awful ... Not one of her own to stand up for her. Probably didn't get a wink of sleep them six days, just stared into space and wished she was back safe in her own corner by the range.

Listen to them down there, pretending everything's grand. It's not fair.

I'm crying again now because I'm remembering the funeral bit. All the huge crowds of people shaking hands and acting normal. Except Mammy. She was the only one right sad. I suppose she was sorry. Thinking about carrying the big case out the path and stuff like that.

Uncle Frank wasn't crying, though. The head of him. If he comes back here again I'll cut his tyres with my penknife, I'll smash his bloody radio.

Please, Granny, don't be mad with me. Or my brother. It wasn't our fault. We couldn't do anything, we couldn't stop them. We were listening at the window but we were afraid. You shouldn't have heeded them. We'd keep coming over to do the jobs for you. Forever. Why did you go? Why, Granny?

Please, God, look after our Granny. Tell her we miss her awful much and if it's not a sin tell her to come down some night and haunt big Uncle Frank. I blame him, but I hope that's not a sin either. Keep Mammy and Daddy quick on the legs and don't let anyone ever, ever, dump them on strangers.

A Fish in Pinstripes

E ddie was painting wrought iron for a couple by the name of Leahy. A balcony job, dead cushy. The one day could do it, no problem, but if he paced himself he might knock two out of it. 2 x £50 = £100, a nice, round number. Folk didn't mind forking out the lolly, Eddie reckoned, once they saw the professional touch. And the Leahys certainly had mucho lolly; everything about the place said so.

It was a scorching morning, the sky a heatwave blue. He hummed snatches of pop songs as he dealt with the tricky curlicues, not a wisp of cloud in his soul. Behind him, the Leahy pad stayed silent, the quietest house he'd ever worked at. Probably still in the sack – or in separate sacks. Eddie, you see, was fond of pressing the fast-forward button on his imagination. Painting could become monotonous, the mind tending to wander. More often than not, it wandered right into the boudoir of fantasy.

Take juicy Stella, for instance. The bossman's missus. It was no pain to send the mind's eye exploring in that territory. A 24-carat stunner. Much as he disliked the briefcased brigade Eddie had to admit that they usually landed lovely wives. Such a waste, he thought, a looker like Stella hidden away in suburbia, not even a bloody pooch for company. Young enough to be the man's daughter, for Christ's sake. Must be bored out of her sexy tree.

When the glass door slid open down at the end of the balcony Eddie assumed an attitude of artistic concentration and toured his brush with great care along the twists of the rails. Looks were everything.

'Well, how is it going?'

He angled his head casually, squinted against the relentless sun.

'Not so bad, sir,' he said. 'Coming along grand.'

Greg Leahy nodded. 'Good, good,' he said, in a less than bothered voice. He flicked spots of dandruff from his pinstriped lapels, fidgeted with the knot of his tie and then stared down into the manicured garden, right down into the fountain where a cherub boldly urinated high into the balmy air.

Eddie kept his brush on the move, kept his eye on the brush.

Greg Leahy started to whistle, stopped abruptly and said: 'Do you think you will get it all done today?'

Eddie rested his brush on the can, studied the length to be painted and fingered his chin. 'I doubt it,' he said. He rose off his knees to take a keener look, his features became a study in concentration. 'No.' He pursed his lips for effect. 'There's two days work there. Wrought iron is slow.'

Greg Leahy lifted his briefcase. 'See how it goes,' he said.

'Sound,' said Eddie, kowtowing back to his work. Within seconds he heard the BMW speed down the tree-lined avenue.

'See you later, boss,' he grinned, rising and fishing his ten-pack from the well of his warm pocket.

At eleven thirty on the dot Eddie broke to drink a mug of sweet tea from his flask. He wasn't a big feeder but he loved the drop of tea.

'What a day,' he thought aloud as he eased over to the suntrap corner by the glass door. He planted himself in a wickerwork chair, one of two that squatted there, just begging to be occupied. Fair play to the Leahys, they like their comforts. He savoured the scent of a cherry tree as it wafted up to him; he regarded the cherub. A grand garden, no doubt. Money talks.

After a few minutes, he unclasped the bib of his overalls, stretched back and welcomed the roasting rays onto his bare chest. Better than the beach, this. He felt like closing the eyes, stealing forty winks, but he repelled the urge. Play his cards right and further morsels of painting might come his way here. Those pillars round the front: flaking. Mmmm.

He was sucking the last out of a second Major, and making to rise, when the glass door slid open and Stella Leahy sauntered past his corner. He did up his bib with quiet haste, killed his butt and stood to attention.

'Oh! ... there you are,' she said, turning. She half smiled, half nodded. She wore a white halter top, and a little wrap-around skirt that reminded Eddie of the birds at Wimbledon. She looked good. Jesus, she looked more than good.

'Just having a cup of tea there,' he said, gesturing without much focus. He edged past her – 'Better do another bit ...' – and stooped to his task.

The hairs of the brush had matted in the sun and the first dip of paint dripped en route to the railing. Lucky he had the sheet spread. He stifled a curse and dipped again. He needed to get his act together pronto because Stella Leahy was showing no signs of shifting – he could see her shadow.

I wish to Christ she'd disappear, he thought, but she didn't disappear.

'It looks lovely,' she said. 'You do a very good job,' she said.

Eddie ventured a slow gaze towards her, withdrew it sharply. She had her palms parked on the cotton knoll of her bum; her legs were tanned and firm. He saw her in the eye of the curlicue; he painted her with a stiff hand.

A few more minutes crawled by. 'See you later,' she said then, in a voice Eddie heard as a come-on. The slowed tone, that trace of huskiness.

She moved out of the corner of his eye. The glass door closed. Stella Leahy was gone but her image lingered, a hot ember in the grate of his groin.

Come three o'clock Eddie was fast running out of railing. His pacing was way off, the brush on automatic pilot. See, for hours he had been acting in and directing his own fantasy. It was busy work, all-consuming.

He sat back on his haunches and ran the heel of his hand along his brow. A ghost eddy of air cooled about him. Blossoms wafted off the cherry tree, one of them landing beside him; he picked it up and absently sniffed it.

Just then, Stella Leahy opened a window on to the balcony, leant out and said: 'Could you come inside a moment, please?'

Eddie jumped to his feet. His heart broke into a trot.

'Could you come round the front … um …'

'Eddie,' he prompted, sensing her struggle to remember his name.

'Yes, of course,' she said. 'Edward,' she said.

He gawked, his brush a lowered weapon, dripping ammo.

'There's a little job I want you to do,' she explained.

No words of response came to him but he did manage a nod, a nod indicative of burden, of bowing to a grim fate. This was real; reality was a minefield.

Stella Leahy left the window, thinking: What a strange chap.

Eddie stayed rooted to his spot. He felt himself smile, one of those nervy smiles that tingle the cheeks. He stared towards the glass door and absently wondered why he couldn't have gone in that way, why she specified the front. He stared down at the pissing cherub. He checked his brow for sweat. He then sucked in fists of air and headed round to do who could say what.

'Good man,' said Stella Leahy when he showed at the front door. 'Leave the brush,' she added. 'It's not painting.'

Eddie gaped at his brush like an amnesiac struggling for recall. He looked about and saw a pot to his right, a pot within which an exotic flower showed its many colours. He bent and balanced the brush on the rim of the pot.

'Come on through.'

After being so long in the dazzle of the sun he felt a touch disoriented when he stepped indoors. The settled dimness, the cave-cool temperature.

'Up here,' said Stella Leahy. She didn't so much climb the spiral stairs as jog her way to the top. Eddie, following at a judicious distance, feasted on the rhythm, the view. She turned left off the landing and started to hum, a humming amplified by the funereal hush of the house.

'Okay,' she said, pausing for a moment before depressing the handle of the master bedroom's door and stealing in. Eddie followed, gnawing at his upper lip. This was dodgy business.

'There's my little problem.' Her tone sounded jaded, resigned, as if this 'problem' was one that had been bothering her for quite a while. Could fish cause a problem? So it seemed, for her gaze was fixed on an aquarium in the far corner of the room.

She ventured closer; she bent, hands planted on knees, and peered into it.

Eddie eyed her pose. He pinched the bridge of his nose. He looked to the waiting bed.

Ten seconds passed, maybe twenty. Nobody was counting.

'A grand fish tank, that,' he remarked.

'Sorry?' said Stella Leahy, straightening, turning blankly towards him. It was only then Eddie grasped that her fixation with the aquarium was genuine. Her eyes said so, their usual sparkle was no more. One thing, and one thing only, was clear: she wasn't contemplating a quick tumble in the sack.

'Just saying it's a grand fish tank,' he repeated. He hid his hands in his pockets and simultaneously flicked his head towards the aquarium, an arching nod.

Stella Leahy let both remark and mime pass, didn't show the merest hint of a response. She looked to the aquarium and bent low, as before.

'There's a fish in there,' she said, shuddering slightly as she spoke.

'A fish,' said Eddie, without any irony whatsoever. See, he wasn't thinking clearly enough to detect the shadow of the absurd in the statement he'd just heard. In fact, he wasn't thinking at all. He was simply standing there in a fancy bedroom, staring at a woman who, in turn, was staring at a fish tank.

'Yes, a fish,' she said, turning once again to face Eddie.

'I see,' he said. Deadpan.

'Oh, what am I saying!' she cried then. She dipped her eyes and inhaled so deeply her nipples stood out. 'You'll probably think I'm crazy,' she began. 'It's …'

'Go on,' encouraged Eddie. He thought to edge closer but held back.

'It's dead, the blasted thing.' She winced on the word 'dead', apparently none too comfortable with things no longer of this world.

'… Oh.'

'Would you, would you mind taking it out for me?'

He looked at her, looked at her. She wasn't biting.

'No problem,' he muttered, moping deflatedly across to the aquarium.

He raised the lid and looked into the water.

'It's over in the corner, by the pump.'

He trawled with a blind hand.

'Wait, let me show you,' said Stella Leahy. She stood alongside Eddie, her hand resting on his shoulder as she craned her head in. He kept cool, hoping the hand would stay. It did stay.

'I have him!' He dragged his fist from the tank, slowly, slowly. He opened it, slowly, slowly, striving for theatrical effect, and revealed the striped and very dead fish to Stella Leahy. He smiled, as if he were presenting her with something nice, something in the line of a gift.

The shell of her trance cracked and a squeal of 'Put it away!' fluttered frantically out. She darted across to the wide bed and perched uneasily, her palms blinkering about her temples. Christ, she was in a right state.

Eddie sniffed the fish: no smell, the fucking thing was too small to have a smell. Where would he put it? Into the back pocket of his overalls.

'You can look now,' he announced. 'He's gone.'

Stella Leahy looked and, after a moment, she smiled: a wee, sheepish smile that was greatly appealing to Eddie. 'Thank you so much, Edward.'

Whether or not she wondered exactly where the fish had gone it was hard to say because she still retained a trace of her earlier abstraction.

Eddie waited. He fiddled with the buckle of his bib, then clasped both hands behind his back and stood erect and firm. He lingered, with the mien of some loyal servant. After a few seconds he felt like a spare prick and decided to head back out.

As he made his exit Stella Leahy muttered: 'I couldn't bear to touch it.'

Eddie stopped dead. 'I know what you're saying,' he said, moving back into the middle of the room. Birdsong trilled in through the open window.

'It's been dead for ages,' she said, as if speaking to her private self.

He studied her and felt a keen urge to sit on that bed. Maybe wing his arm round her, offer a bit of comfort. See how it went from there.

'My husband never noticed. I hadn't the heart to tell him.'

'I understand. It's not easy.'

'No,' said Stella Leahy. 'Nooo.' She twisted her thick gold ring round and round her finger – the way certain women have a habit of doing when lost in thought. Her eyes livened finally and travelled back to the aquarium.

'I'll have to tell him now, though.'

'Sure you can always get another one,' suggested Eddie. He inched closer.

'I know,' said Stella Leahy in an oddly stern voice.

They both eyed the aquarium; the lid was still up.

'What did you call him?' Eddie asked, trying to inject some measure of compassion, of pathos, into his voice.

Stella Leahy stared at him.

'The-the-fish,' he stuttered. He realized he was floundering but he had to plough on, he had nothing to lose. 'What was his name?'

She upped from the bed. 'It was a fish, Edward. We're talking about a fish here, just a pathetic fish.' Her tone was dismissive, coloured with scorn. She gestured him from the room and off he went, his fantasy dashed.

Down at the front door, his hand on the brass knob, he heard her thank him again and, without turning, he grumbled: 'It was nothing.'

But then he heard a cry that offered fresh promise: 'Wait! Come back!'

He turned. He readied himself.

'Where did you put it? The fish! Where did you leave it?'

'Oh … the fish. He's in here.'

He fished the fish out of his pocket and dropped it into the plate of his other hand. Stella Leahy's features registered instant and complex disgust.

'Get rid of it,' she said, waving Eddie and the fish away. 'Throw it in the fountain, throw it anydamnwhere.' She turned on her heel, her scent wafting.

By the time he got back to the balcony Eddie Jones had already sucked half a Major into his lungs. Boy, did he need that cigarette badly. He leant on the railings and gazed out across the garden, puffing away, not giving a continental fuck whether her ladyship saw him or not. The woman was bonkers.

Soon he was leaking sweat. He lit another Major, his senses back indoors. He blew a smoke ring and replayed the crazy video, editing as he went.

There's my little problem, said Stella Leahy as he floated over the carpet and started to massage the contours of her luscious form. Stop it, she said. It's a fish, she said. They were on the bed, the soft, swimming bed. Don't stop, she said. Please don't stop, Edward, she said.

A blur of blossoms wafted from the cherry tree.

'Ed-ward,' called Stella Leahy from the corner of the balcony.

Eddie spun round, coughing on smoke. He saw she'd dolled herself up to the nines. That was fast, he thought. 'I'm popping out for a while. Greg shall look after you when he gets home. Byee!' She turned and sped down the steps, the song of her stilettos singing on stone.

The Lancia's sleek body scintillated through the linden trees as it zoomed out the avenue and stopped dead beyond the rattled ramp. A few seconds' wait for traffic clearance, a few impatient revs, and then Stella Leahy was away, her fish forgotten.

She's not off shopping, that's for sure, Eddie mused. Not in that gear. He butted his cigarette, cast an eye at his watch, and bent to give the can of paint a wee stir. Instantly, he felt a chilly kiss on the left cheek of his arse. He straightened and fished out the fish. It was slimy to touch but Eddie wasn't bothered by slime. He pinched its tail between thumb and forefinger, held it aloft and regarded it with forensic detachment. The striped skin, that was unusual. Or maybe it wasn't, he knew fuck-all about fish. Throw it in the fountain, throw it anydamnwhere. He grinned. 'Greg,' he said, 'you should have been called Greg. A fish in pinstripes!' He gnawed at his upper lip and kept grinning. He looked towards the pissing cherub, took aim and flicked. 'I couldn't bear to touch it,' he mimicked. Laughter welled up in him, warm waves of laughter breaking over the balcony, flooding down into the manicured garden. 'I couldn't bear to touch it,' he cried again, his face contorting into a screw of delight.

Several minutes passed before he could compose himself and focus on paint. Then he remembered he'd left his brush around at the front, beside the door, beside the exotic flower. He strolled off to retrieve it, his step light as a dancer, the birds of suburbia trilling in his heart.

Dead Fathers

I wanted a woman. Or maybe I didn't but when I saw her sitting on her own in the corner I wandered over. It started some way like that.

She was around the thirty mark, and plain. A slouched and weary posture. Her nervy eyes dipped as I wavered beside her, her whole frame went taut.

Whatever lines I used, they seemed to work because she quickly responded in a welcoming manner. Even pulled up a stool for me. I saw she, too, was hitting the lager, a stack of empties on the low table. My brother watched from the bar: pole-straight, observing my moves. His sober stare.

The pounding music and the crowd buzz soon faded away, leaving me and the woman adrift out on the periphery. Just me, the woman, and the cool lager. We talked a bit, or at least she talked. Her voice a drone in the swamp of my brain.

She stank of perfume. A kind of dying-roses smell. Coming in wafts. What the hell took me over to her? She didn't attract me, drunk and all as I was. I suppose she didn't attract anybody. Trapped there in that corner, watching but not being watched. Another sad story.

I made flattering remarks on her appearance. Stuff about her clothes and hair. I think I may even have said I liked her perfume. Jesus Christ!

A mate of mine gave me a wink on his way to the cigarette machine. A slow wink. Male. Approving. I could imagine how he saw the thing.

I curved an eye onto the woman's legs. Flesh-coloured stockings. Tights? That's right, they were tights. Nicely-shaped legs, scissored always.

Suddenly, she was rambling on about something, and starting to sniffle. 'Father' and 'died' were two words I isolated and straight away those two words made me leave my drink down, stung me into momentary sobriety.

'What'd you say …?' I asked, and she repeated it. Her bony hand reached often for the lager but as soon as the white fingers would be tight around the glass they'd loosen and pull away. Then she'd push her palm forcefully along her skirt, along her hidden thigh. It was so annoying, that.

'I understand,' I said finally, when a long silence told me she must be finished. 'My own father died too … Six months ago.' I took a huge gulp of the lager and squeezed my hand around hers.

'Stop it,' she said. 'I'm serious,' she said. She broke away from me, her arms wrapping, straitjacket-fashion, about her skinny frame.

'No-no, it's true,' I insisted, my voice all hard-edged.

She looked searchingly at me and, with some effort, I held her gaze. So striking, those eyes of hers. Green pools. A tremendous vivid green.

I reached out my hand again. Touched her on shoulder and then on the elbow. Gently, sympathetically. Her arms came loose, her clammy hand tentatively meeting mine. I squeezed it to reassure her, spoke a few kind words. She just stared away into the crowd, a fiercely lost stare.

I studied her closer then. The bone profile. A glimpse of her bra strap: black against the silky white blouse. Pendant with silver cross.

Suddenly, she jerked her head round, caught me unawares. Those eyes.

I tried to adopt the appropriate look as she started into the sniffling again. Her lips trembled as she raved on and on. She made to pull her hand free but I held it tight, wouldn't let its strange comfort escape.

'I know,' I said through clenched teeth. 'It's hard.'

I wished to Christ she'd stop. It was getting to me, having to listen to all this stuff about her father. I tried to slip the mood but failed.

'How … how did he die?' I said finally. My voice low, my eyes dipping. A beer mat on the wet table read: 'HARP – The bite of the night'. Her trapped hand clawed instinctively as the word 'cancer' came out in a taut whisper. I, too, muttered the word, a chill instantly icing along my spine. In that bonding moment, I wanted both to run away from her and to hold her close.

Only when she started to really sob did I look up from the beer mat and meet her eyes, eyes now spilling tears.

'It's okay,' I soothed, drawing her into my arms. 'Sshh, you're okay.'

Gaping over her shoulder, I saw a couple kissing in the far shadows. The lad's hand was up the girl's jumper. She seemed to tug at his curly hair.

I closed my eyes, squeezed them shut. We were swaying as one. I felt her tears hot on my jawbone. Her hair smelt of a dandruff shampoo I once used.

The vulnerability of her body, its tragic shuddering, melted something deep inside me and I began to tour my hands comfortingly about her back. The feel of her through the flimsy blouse quickly sabotaged my senses. I was about to kiss the slender curve of her neck, or maybe I was just imagining doing so, when she loosed herself from my needy hold and edged away a bit.

She got the sobbing stopped and searched for a dry part of the tissue to fix up her ruined face. I lifted my glass and sighed into it, then gulped. When I forced my head round she was again staring at me, trying bravely to smile. A lock of hair stuck to her cheek, red as a new wound.

'I'm sorry,' she said. 'I didn't mean to … It's the drink … Sorry …'

Once more I offered her my hand. She hesitated for a long moment before accepting it, clenching it. The quiet firmness of her grip surprised me.

She slipped in closer when stretching for her glass. She stayed close. I thumbed the damp lock behind her ear as she drank the lager. My hand lingered in her hair and I nodded a smile. She smiled too, freely, without pain.

Her eyes, though, still unnerved me. So focused, as if reading secrets in my head. I tried to think of the right words to say but no words came.

When she started to speak again I reached sharply for my drink.

'Here I am making a scene before a total stranger and –'

'Tony,' I said. I left my glass down. 'My name is Tony.'

'I'm Regina,' she said. The voice suddenly innocent. Childlike almost.

We shook hands then, having to untwine our fingers to do so. She grinned sheepishly at this awkward linkage, looking oddly lovely as she did so.

'Tony, I'm so sorry … for crying like that.' She broke off to sip at her lager before continuing: 'You must think of your father a lot too?'

'I do,' I said. 'I do ...' I made to say her name but it was gone. Blank.

A moment later my mind seemed to shift, and then I did think of my father. It swept over me, all the blocked-out past. Beyond chronology, breaching the dam of lager, a torrent of fleeting but poignant rememberings. Sitting safe on the bar of his high Raleigh ... threats of giving me the door when I reeled in drunk at seventeen ... tramping cocks in the buttoms ... reading him the fight reports from the papers, Ali and Joe Frazier ... taken home by a cop in the dead of night after wrecking my Honda 50 ... his hooded gaze as I left for the boat, that unforgettable stare. And then I saw him at the end, even smelt the flowers in his hospice room. The way he gazed at me through death-steady, fading eyes, struggling for last words but weighed down by morphine ...

'Tony, oh Tony,' said the woman, sensing my burden. She crawled her hand round on the curve of my back, up to the nape of my neck. Both of us sighed then and gazed off into the alien crowd, into our private and unsharable voids. Her fondling fingers felt good; remote but so, so good.

Fresh drinks. Silver reeling from my fist onto the table.

My eyes and the woman's eyes meeting, locking.

I attack the lager, a trickle of it cooling through my shirt-front.

'You won't get more,' she says as I make to rise. 'The shutters are long down.' She pushes her own untouched pint across to me. I nod heavily.

'Time to go home, folks! Come on! Come on! It's way after time!'

I force my head around. Stools on the low tables. Brother gone, everyone gone. Just me and the woman. And the fat barman, mopping close.

'I'll walk you home ...' My voice low, a whisper. Still aware. The barman swiping our glassses, muttering, rocking his oily head.

His straight whistle as we stand and steer a path out into the night.

I wake in the woman's warm bed. She is not by my side. I settle an eye on my watch: half ten. I'm bursting for a piss, my throat is parched. Staring over at the closed door I listen for sounds from the kitchen or footsteps. No sound reaches my ear, the silence is total. A few minutes pass, muddled minutes. Gradually, street echoes steal in and become individualized. The common groan of traffic; fired greetings; the juddering of a distant jackhammer. Wonder is she gone off out? I try to recall her name. I trawl back through the night, back through the lurking shadows. I see us sprawled on the settee … the vodka … the stereo playing country-and-western dirges. I mull over later doings as I continue to gape at the closed door. The jack-hammer is getting louder.

Then it hits me like a flash that she talked of rising early for work.

My clothes are scattered by the bed and hastily I get into them. I cross to the rainy window and find my bearings. There's a lorry idling nearby, the thumps of heavy stuff being unloaded. Everyone has an umbrella up.

Just as I turn for the door I spot the note on the bedside locker.

I feel my pulse start to quicken, a shortness of breath.

Tony,

It's eight and I'm off. You are dead to the world and I don't have the heart to wake you. Maybe you might give me a ring later today? I work across in Gunn's (you know the accountancy place?). Fix yourself a bite to eat before you go – if your stomach is up to it! Must head. Bye. Bye. Bye.

Regina.

I read it twice, three times. The tone is so casual, so … nice. I feel a severe stab of guilt. Regina. I say the same aloud, and sniff at the pinky paper. Fresh snatches of the night whisper through to me, then hit hard as belly blows. I sigh shakily and stare at the rumpled bed, stare all round the room, before replacing the note on the locker and making for the door.

The hall is shockingly unfamiliar. Straight away I see the telephone but I ignore it and go in search of liquid. I eye the settee, run my fingers along its upholstery as I continue on into the kitchen. A few tumblers of metal-tangy water, then a long leak in the bathroom, and vague thoughts of going for a cure in The Black Sheep on my way home.

Yet when I return to the main room I linger, even flop into the settee.

Something seems to be holding me, some unresolved notion or whatever. I notice the vodka glasses are still on the carpet: a drop in one, the other toppled. I also notice Regina's stilettos over near the stereo. It's crazy but I suddenly feel at ease, a rare comfort shawling about me. What if she came in the door? What then?

And still I remain in the soft dip of the settee.

After a minute or two I rise, breathe in the room's smell and wander over to have a look at myself in the sideboard's mirror. It's then I see, there amidst the silver and glass and shrivelled daffodils, the oval photograph.

I lift it, instantly feeling a lump form in my throat. Regina is smiling girlishly, her right arm draped round the shoulders of a rangy man who I'm certain is her father. Her face so fresh and untroubled. She wears a plain but elegant sleeveless dress; also a stole, and a broad-brimmed hat tilted sharply. She looks great. Her father stares out through countryman eyes, awkward before the camera, yet so obviously proud in that tender moment. A carnation in his lapel suggests the snap was taken at a family wedding. I can't stop looking at it; I even find my fingers brushing the cold glass.

A fresh sense of loss takes root in me, keener and more focused than in the boozed night. It quickly becomes overwhelming, heavy as a stone in my heart. There are no captured moments of me with my father; there's no draped arm. Memories, that's all. The images from childhood too perfect and painful to relive now; the strained years of my coming-of-age, of our slow estrangement. Death-bed tears when it was too late, when there remained only the frozen truth of missed opportunity.

I avoid my reflection in the polished mirror as I tremble the photograph back to its spot and turn away. The silence is solid as a wall.

I push out to the hallway and sink onto the stool beside the phone. I feel so alone, so dreadfully adrift. I remember back to the night, grasp at its small and transient comforts. Minutes pass. I lift the directory and leaf through it, finally locating Gunn's. Almost without any spur of will, I dial the number, then hang up on the first ring. I hug myself and stare at the bare, white wall. I think to leave but instead I dial again. A man answers and I ask for Regina. I'm still staring at the wall when she comes on the line. 'Hello?' she says, her voice dim, the voice of a stranger. 'Tony ... is that you ...?' I cannot respond; I feel numbed, unconnected. I lower the receiver from my ear, it trembles like a living thing. The voice continues to echo, speaking my name over and over. I listen to it until it is no more, until the line goes dead and a new voice calls to me through the silence.

'Daddy,' I hear myself whisper as I hang up, rise and mope blindly away.

'Oh Christ, Daddy ...'

Pandora's Box

He was a good forty metres past her when his foot pounced on the brake pedal and brought the swift Audi to a halt. He eyed the hitcher in his rear-view mirror, noticed her indecision. He thought to reverse but palmed the horn instead. Yes, she was coming. He adjusted the mirror a fraction to take in her steady approach.

The hitcher opened the door and peered in. 'Hi,' she said, two-handing a cascade of hair behind her ears as she ran a mental check on the driver.

'Hop in.'

'How far are you headed?'

'Cork. All the way to Cork.'

'Yeah, okay!' she decided, and she made to get in.

'Throw the knapsack in the back.' He signaled, as if heading a ball.

It was ten minutes since he'd picked up the hitcher and few words of consequence had been exchanged – small talk, the normal stuff. He fidgeted with the radio buttons as if seeking some new station, some diverse sound. Finally he returned the dial to its old mark and hit the 'off'.

The Audi surged towards ninety as he fished in his pockets for cigarettes and steered one between his lips. This was another rule he was about to break; besides lifting hitchhikers, which he never did, he was now going to start smoking while driving. He hesitated but then his thumb moved sharply to engage the car's lighter.

'Smoke?' he said, showing the open packet of Dunhills.

'Ahm, is it okay?' She meant the No Smoking sticker and he knew this.

'It's okay. Work away, it's okay,'

'I'll go for one of my own.' She pulled a pouch of Drum from the breast pocket of her lumberjack shirt and started to make a roll-up. She was good at the job, real handy.

'Fair enough,' he said, a peeled eye settling back on the road.

'Thanks all the same. I appreciate it.'

The Audi eased back to seventy but soon the speedo needle was creeping again towards dangerous figures. The driver tapped a pellet of ash onto the floor and then he pulled open the ashtray and used that. It was packed with his wife's butts from the last time she'd accompanied him on a drive to Galway.

'Gawd, the countryside looks magical,' the hitcher said, her eyes drawn by a pair of frisky chestnuts galloping in an isolated paddock.

The driver stared straight ahead, the great flats of road melting into mirages. The speedo now said a steady eighty.

'What part of America would you be from?' he asked suddenly.

'Georgia,' said the hitcher. 'Athens, Georgia.'

'Athens … Georgia …' he repeated.

'You got it.'

'Now that doesn't sound American to me.'

'Well. It sure is. Don't ask me how it came to be called that because I ain't got a clue.'

'Something to do with the Greeks, maybe.'

'I guess so.'

The Audi slowed as it hit the outskirts of Cashel and the driver rolled his window down, rolled it right down, sent his arm out into the sun.

'You see that up there?' he said, pointing towards the imposing fortress which lorded a local hill. 'That's the Rock of Cashel.'

'Uh-huh.'

'It's famous, you know.'

'I bet,' said the American, using her hitching sign to fan her face. He brought the Audi down another gear and gazed up at the Rock – almost as if he were the tourist.

'Do you want to take a photo of it?' he said. 'I can stop. No problem.'

'Not really,' said the American in a tired drawl. 'I ain't much into all that dead stuff. You understand?'

'I do, I know what you're saying,' he said, rolling his window slowly shut before pushing the Audi into a higher gear.

The snug town of Cashel seemed to shimmer in the midday heat. The driver kept the Audi at a crawl, his fingers interlocked, prayer-fashion, atop the padded steering wheel, his eyes scouring left and right.

'Cashel,' he said. 'This is the town of Cashel.'

'Downtown Cashel,' said the American.

He glanced across at her and smiled weakly.

Leaving the town of Cashel behind, they moved on through the fertile pastures of dairy country and the driver lit another Dunhill. He drove in silence now, his eyes fixed on the bad bends.

He thumbed the radio back on and a woman could be heard talking about the private life of Mozart. He got a pop station. He switched off.

'You're very quiet there,' he said.

'Yeah,' said the American. 'I guess I'm a bit … what is it you folks say? Wrecked.'

'I see,' said the driver, directing his eyes back to the snaky road.

'And stuff,' she added.

'Do you have a name?'

'Sure I have a name. You want to know it?'

'It would help.'

'Marilyn. Marilyn Goldwater.'

'Goldwater.'

'That's the one.'

'Goldwater … Goldwater. Wasn't there a politician –'

'Yeah-yeah,' she cut in.

'You wouldn't be …?'

'Nope. No kin to me. Never knew him, never wanted to know him.'

'A gangster was he?'

'Dunno. Who cares? Who cares about all that stuff?'

'Hmmm. I suppose you're right,' said the driver. He eased down through the gears and indicated to pass a lorry that was stacked high with baled straw.

'A student, are you?'

Marilyn inhaled deeply and gazed at the padded roof of the car.

'A student?' she said. 'Yeah, I guess you could say I'm a student.'

He took a hand off the wheel and wiped it on his kneecap. The load of golden straw grew smaller and smaller as he watched it in his rear-view mirror.

'Have you friends or something in Cork?'

'Can't say I do.'

'You'll like it. A grand spot is Cork. A grand spot,' he repeated, angling his hairy wrist just enough to show the face of his watch.

Marilyn set to making a roll-up, her head swaying ever so slightly to a private beat. The driver sent an eyeball left. He saw the faded jeans, a sunflower patch on her near thigh. He saw her tongue the cigarette paper.

'You wanna try one of these?' she asked.

'No-no,' he said. 'No.'

'I can roll you one.'

'You're all right, work away,' he said. 'There wouldn't be drugs in that now?' he asked a few moments later.

'Just good ol' Golden Virginia.'

'The drugs are a queer boy.'

'A queer boy!' cried Marilyn. She burst into giggles, coughed on smoke.

A long silence followed. The driver wiped an imaginary eel of sweat from his lined brow and then he asked Marilyn if she slept in a tent. 'When you're touring like this, I mean,' he explained.

'Hostels,' she said. 'I prefer to use the youth hostel.'

'All bunked in together, I suppose.'

'Sorry?'

'In those places. Would the lads and lassies be together, like?'

Marilyn Goldwater worried the Indian beads about her throat.

'Yeah, I guess they could end up together,' she said. 'Do you have a problem with that?'

'No. No.'

'That's okay then.'

'That's right.'

He reached for another Dunhill.

'Sure, I know,' said Marilyn, a teasing Irish lilt to her voice. She comforted herself deeper into the Audi's soft seat and lifted a sandalled foot onto the bare shelf of the dashboard.

'Just asking,' said the driver. He jetted smoke from the corner of his mouth and veered a peripheral eye onto the roosting foot.

'Sure. You're just curious. Right?'

'Not curious, just asking. Nothing wrong with that?'

'It's a free world, man, a free world.'

'Someone has to pay for it, though,' he said.

He tamped his half-smoked Dunhill into the packed ashtray, instantly wishing he hadn't.

'Pay for it? Pay for what?'

'You know what I mean.'

'No, honestly. Come on.'

'Everything,' said the driver. 'Everything.'

A few miles before Mitchelstown, Marilyn started to hum a snatch of an old Carole King song. Very low, very sweet. She smiled dreamily as she hummed, the smile of a traveller making good time. 'Are you married?' she asked suddenly.

'Am I married?' he said, stunned.

'Yeah. Don't mean to be personal or anything.'

'I am,' he said with slight hesitation. He looked back at the road and saw another mirage in the distance, a melt of phantom water.

'Why do you ask?' he said, after a few long seconds.

'Dunno,' said Marilyn. 'To quote you, I was just asking,' she laughed.

'You're not married yourself, I suppose?'

'Nope. I sure ain't.'

'I thought that.'

'It works for some, it don't work for some. I ain't the gambling type.'

'I see.'

'Too much pressure. Too much space for lies and hurting.'

'How? What do you mean exactly?' His tone was challenging.

Marilyn raised her foot above the dashboard, settled it back down again.

'Go on, I'm interested.'

'I ain't got the energy,' she said languidly but with an undertone of annoyance. 'Not today. Sorry.' She teased a bit of tobacco from her pouch, evened it deftly along the paper and gazed out at a shimmering hillside of tremendous colour – a crop of rapeseed ready for the shiny blades.

'We could pull for a drink up ahead,' he ventured. 'It's roasting.'

'Sure, if you want,' said Marilyn, 'but I gotta be pushing on for Cork.'

'Just a quick drink.'

'Thanks for the offer but I gotta pass on it.'

'Whatever you say. Just asking.'

'I know,' said Marilyn, studying the finished roll-up abstractedly.

The Audi devoured the good road into Mitchelstown, the purr of its engine hardening towards a whine. The speedo needle was hovering about the eighty-five mark when the driver sucked the last out of his last cigarette. His left hand dropped onto the gear shift.

He brought the car to a halt in the centre of town, thumbed the hazard flashers on and unbuckled his seat-belt.

'Won't be a minute,' he said. 'Just going to get fags.'

Back outside the shop he stood in the shade of the awning and lit a Major – they didn't stock Dunhill. He gazed down the street for long private seconds, eyes focused on his car with the blinking hazards. He tossed the cigarette aside then and strode forward, viewing his reflection in a butcher's window as he went.

'Now,' he said, sitting in and belting up.

'Nice little town,' said Marilyn.

'Mitchelstown,' he said, as he eased the Audi away.

'I guess we're in Cork already.'

'What? What do you mean guess?'

'In the county. Somewhere in the county. Right?'

'Aye, aye,' he said testily. 'The very north,' he added a moment later, his tone softer, grudgingly apologetic.

On the twisting incline out of the town, a heavily laden lorry slowed the Audi to a crawl.

'Come on, come on,' he said to the lorry, pulling the cigarettes out of his pocket and stabbing one between his lips.

'Here,' he said to Marilyn. 'Try one of these.'

'It's okay, I'm fine.'

'Come on, come on,' he said to the lorry again. He nosed out and in, out and in, mad for road.

'I guess it's going as fast as it can,' said Marilyn. 'Whatever's under that canvas sure must be heavy.'

The driver kept a still eye in his wing mirror as the lorry groaned on up the hill, gear changes punctuating its smoky climb.

'Pandora ...' thought Marilyn aloud.

'What?'

'Pandora,' she said again, pointing. 'The sign on the truck. See?'

'Hmm.'

'Strange name for a haulage company. Maybe that's why it's labouring so hard.'

She chuckled after a moment.

He gaped across at her, his face a taut mask of blankness.

'Pandora's Box,' she explained. 'You know the one. The huge weight of all those miseries and dreads and stuff waiting to break free. I –'

The sudden swerve and thrust of the Audi cut Marilyn's drawl; the lorry was quickly left far behind as the open road beckoned. The driver powered up through the gears, his jaw set hard. The speedo needle hit ninety, kept on going; the blossomed whitethorns became woolly spectres of the margins.

'Are you afraid?'

'Afraid of what?'

'Of speed.'

'Naw, not a bit,' said Marilyn. 'I get a hit off speed.'

'She's only cruising, you know. This lady has a lot more in the tank.'

'Sure.'

'Cruising,' he repeated through viced teeth. 'Only cruising.'

Keep hitting the gas, mister, she thought. You're doing real fine. She smoked a roll-up, her cheek nesting against the wing of the seat. It was such a comfortable car; the hum of its engine settled about her brain. Had she not been so fatigued, she would have reopened the channel of conversation – if only for kicks. As it was, she thought of Cork.

Cork: she liked its single-syllable roundness.

The driver, meanwhile, thanked Christ the law weren't out with a speed trap and now took it cautious and slow: a steady fifty. He didn't look at his passenger, nor in his rear-view or wing mirrors, didn't look anywhere but at the road ahead. He imagined Marilyn having a muted giggle, pitying him maybe. Just a quick drink. Whatever you say. Just asking. And the car, it was so fucking hot. He teased loose the noose of his tie and made to wind his window down but stopped.

Her smell, that's what stopped him. So long he'd been breathing it in, unaware. He was aware of it now, wouldn't let it escape or be diluted.

Her cedarwood-oil scent lured his every sense.

'You're getting the weather anyway,' he heard himself say, his voice all shackled, without fluidity.

No response issued from the so-close seat.

'It makes all the difference,' he continued. 'Nothing to beat the bit of …'

Three or four telegraph poles of silence flashed by before he angled his gaze left. The hitcher was fast asleep, a sleep so quiet her very breathing seemed suspended. Her roll-up, half smoked but now gone out, horned from the fold of her limp fingers; her foot slept high on the dashboard, naked inside its sandal.

The Audi eased back to forty, thirty, slowed to twenty where it began to jolt in need of a lower gear.

Wake up, wake up, he pleaded mutely.

He came to a picnic area on the rim of a wood and he saw knots of people seated at the ash-slab tables and he kept going. A juggernaut droned past, horn booming, its slipstream pressing down on the crawling Audi.

He ran his palm across his brow but there was no sweat there.

Jesus, he whispered.

He stared across at the hitcher.

Jesus, he said again.

The speedometer said forty when he looked at it. He checked what gear he was in. He pushed the Audi up to sixty, was afraid to go faster. On the straight coming into Fermoy he forced an eye to his left but drew it back sharply. Again he palmed his brow for sweat. He thumbed the radio on. He turned the volume up, turned it right up, then lowered it.

'Wha-wha?' cried Marilyn Goldwater, starting awake. '… Oh …'

She whipped her foot off the dashboard and peered at her watch and suddenly looked across at the silent driver.

'Gawd,' she said, 'I can't believe I … Where exactly are we …?'

'Fermoy.'

She stared out the window. She wanted to ask how close they were to Cork but didn't.

'I'm real sorry about dropping off like that. Anti-social, I guess.'

He said nothing.

Hitting Fermoy, the Audi slowed and stayed slow. Duffy's

Amusements were in town – the roller-coaster going full tilt in the fairground – but the driver had eyes only for the central junction up ahead.

'I have to let you out here,' he said, pulling sharply in to the side, grimacing as he felt a hub-cap graze off the high kerb.

'Oh?' said Marilyn, glancing across. 'Yeah … okay.'

She saw the set of his jaw, the way his hands clawed the steering wheel. 'Thanks anyway,' she offered, feeling for the clasp of the seat-belt.

'I can't bring you further.'

'Sure,' she muttered, pushing open the door. 'That's okay.'

The driver's grim gaze stayed fixed on the junction.

Marilyn eyed the back of his head as she leant into the rear of the Audi and yanked her rucksack out onto the pavement. She stepped forward a pace to the front door. 'Thanks again,' she said, hands tight on her thighs as she stooped to look in. Nothing from the driver, nothing at all. She shrugged, and eased the door quietly shut – almost as if being careful not to rouse the figure within.

The Audi inched away, quickly gained speed. It shot through the junction in a jangle of gears and followed the main road towards Cork. She drifted after it, her blond head rocking, weighted with puzzlement, rocking until the car's whine faded and another slowed to a halt before her absently rising thumb.

Home Cooking

He'll be here soon and I still can't bring meself to do it. I tried, I did try. Got him out of the sink and all, on to the draining board. I used two Quinnsworth bags for gloves. I even went as far as getting the flick knife and shooting the blade out and pointing it at his belly. But that was it, I could go no further. Them glassy eyes, staring at me like he was alive. And the pong off him. Eventually, I gave up. Giving me the creeps he was.

If only he hadn't caught the shagging brute. Him and his bleeding rod. I get the shivers, just thinking how awful it turned out. I do, I'm serious. It's me own fault so it is because I was mad excited to go. I thought it would be nice out at the lake, thought we might do something else after he got bored with the fishing. Maybe go for a walk, pick flowers and that. So peaceful it was at first, the silence massive. Not a sound except the plops as the steel bait landed far out in the water. I liked it. I started to imagine what it must be like to be a culchie. I smoked a few fags. Johnny seemed calm. Softer. As if he'd escaped from some secret trouble.

I must've been a million miles away when his voice suddenly shook me. 'I have a big one,' he said, all excited. 'A fucking monster.' The rod curved so much I was sure it would snap. The muscle in his left arm, where one of his tattoos is, bulged till it looked like a solid ball with a dragon on it. 'Stay back!' he yelled when I tried to help him pull. A real big yell, so loud it made a whitish bird shoot up from the far side of the lake and away like the clappers. A few seconds later this huge fish burst through the water and flopped back down. Such a splash! Johnny kept on reeling and then he warned me again, although I wasn't getting in his way or nothing.

I don't know how long passed – ages it seemed – before there was another splash near the edge, a little ripply one this time. I could see him plain now, turned over on his side, knackered. Johnny jerked the line hard and suddenly the damn fish flew up and out behind us. Way over our heads, nearly like a scene from a cartoon. There were stones where he landed.

If he was alive when he got tugged from the water I was sure the stones would put a finish to him. Bust his brains out. But no. Away into the jumping with him, alive as meself.

Johnny dropped the rod. 'A stone, gimme a stone,' he said. As if I was a shagging maid. I knew why he wanted a stone, and it made me feel sick, but I went to get one anyway – keeping me eye well clear of the monster.

'A stone, not a shagging pebble!' He found a bigger one, way bigger, one that made him use both hands to lift. The fish wasn't jumping as much now, nearer to dying. Even so, Johnny couldn't wait.

The first stone he flung missed but 'twasn't long till there was another bombing in and that didn't miss. And then another and another and another. He was panting real hard, cursing too. Cursing the fish. Saying: 'Die, for fuck's sake. Die, ya bastard.' I was grinning as I watched him but not the funny kind of a grin. Just me nerves, I suppose. There was nothing one bit funny. Johnny's eyes were bulged and glassy, his face had gone white as a sheet. That fish must have terrified him in some strange way, or reminded him of something he hated. By maybe the seventh stone, there was no more jumping, but even then Johnny wasn't on for getting up too close.

'He's dead at last,' he said. He eyed me in the scaryish but kinda sad way and after a second he smiled. That smile of his, it always gets me. I ran over and threw me arms around him. His whole body felt stiff and trembly, I could feel his heart hammering in me ear. Then he half laughed and half pushed me away, the tough biker again. I felt awful, just bleeding awful.

'Some pike,' he said, hunkering down beside the monster. 'Must be a good ten pounds.' He went to lift him but then jerked his hands away, nearly as if he thought the razory teeth could still rip into his flesh. I was going to make a smart comment but I stopped meself. See, I felt suddenly afraid. Afraid of Johnny, like. I still can't explain that, though I thought about it loads today. It's doing me head.

He finally got enough courage to touch the fish and then a dig the hook out with his flick knife. There was blood on his hands when he'd finished and it made me feel shivery inside. Like swallowing ice. I bit me lip when he stood, I prayed he'd do no more casting. I couldn't bear the thought of any more.

All the quiet closing in on me; waiting for that sudden explosion in the water. Boy, was I glad when he said about us heading back. Like jelly me legs were, even worse than when we used to be doing it in the bushes by the canal and his tongue half way down me throat.

There was no talk as we hurried up the hill to the place where he'd left the bike. Big drops of rain were falling, the sky turning all purplish and dirty, not one patch of blue left. I wouldn't hold his hand although a bit of me wanted to. It was hard enough just to walk beside him and to imagine the disgusting thing in his bag, it being brought home and into our gaff.

I don't know what I'd have done this morning only for I had Ma to go to. It wasn't easy to head over there, seeing how I've been dodging her since me and Johnny got this gaff. A whole month and not a single sight of me in The Towers. She's still me Ma, though.

'So, he turned rough, did he?' she says, the second I'm in the door. No hello or nothing. But I knew when she offered me a fag that she was worried. 'Twas an early hour for me to be on the go, and I'm sure I didn't look the best, seeing how I slept bad and that. I told her about the lake, and then what Johnny was expecting me to do, but she only laughed. Laughed her bleeding head off. She still sees me as a kid – and me near seventeen! The laughing soon turned to seriousness, and a new pack of fags appeared, and we had a good talk. She's wise, I have to say that for her. And tough, too. Hard as nails after going through so much crap before Da fucked off.

She fried burgers later on and was awful nice, even pushed a fiver on me when I was leaving. I was like a zombie, moping back, thinking of all she said about pike, how rotten they were, and thinking how Johnny would go spare if I didn't have a feed of it ready for him.

Just five shagging fags left. Better hold on to a few …

If only some of me mates'd call up. Tanya, next door, was no help, never even heard of pike. Jesus, you'd feel sorry for her. The way she just sits there, her eyes away in another world, her belly bleeding massive.

I often hear her crying and then I can't stop meself from putting an ear close to the wall. Listening. Nearly crying with her. At times like that I wish Johnny would zoom home so I could hold him, feel his strong arms round me.

He's not into softness now, though, not like he used to be in the start. Except when we're in bed and that. Cuddling. Though he can be rough there, too, sometimes. Forcing me to do things I don't like. Afterwards, when I'm still wide awake and he's snoring beside me, I often drift away and see a picture of Tanya. Not a real picture, like, just in me head. Frozen beyond the thin wall, smoking, maybe thinking of how her fella pissed off. Still, the little baby should soon arrive. That'd get her out of the dumps. I bet she'll call it Mel if it's a boy. After Mel Gibson, the hunk in the *Lethal Weapon* film. Loads of his posters all over her gaff. He's lovely so he is, them sparkly eyes.

Johnny won't stand for any famous fellas on our walls, hates them so he does. I still shiver when I think of the evening he came home and me after putting up me favourite one of Bryan Adams. I put it up partly to cover a splodge of damp but there was no point in telling Johnny that. 'Who's this fucking wimp!' he roared, pulling it down and ripping it to shreds. I felt afraid of him then for the first time. His eyes turned vicious, just like at the lake yesterday evening. I had to look away. The next thing, I heard the door bang and he was gone. Never came back till all hours, and me half crazy thinking he'd hit the cider with his mates. He didn't, though. I was in bed, pretending to be asleep, but I knew he wasn't high. He just crept in beside me, dead quiet, and lay on his back like a stiff. Sorry, maybe.

Sometimes I wish we'd stayed as we were and not bothered with this fucking gaff. It was different before, kinda new every time we'd meet. Something to look forward to when I'd be daydreaming in front of the telly or out on the balcony staring at the junkies coming and going down below.

Still, Johnny is me own special fella and I know he loves me. He doesn't say it, not any more, but he does love me. I don't care what anyone says.

I'll never forget the time I first spotted him hanging round the arcade. He'd pull up on his flash Yamaha and start revving it. Showing off, like. Then he'd mosey in, real slow. True as God! He looked heavy in his leathers, dead tough. They all fancied him, even me best mate, Shar. Giggling and giving him the eye. He'd mess about a bit, kissing and that, but never bring anyone off. A few weeks passed before he spoke to me but I knew all along I was the one he really wanted. I just felt it. It was a Saturday night when he beckoned me over and asked me to come for a spin. Me belly went all funny but before I knew right what was happening I jumped on his high saddle and away we went like a rocket. No helmet or nothing – and me denim skirt creeping up to me bleeding fanny! The wind rushing through me hair, cooling me legs, everything flying past in a blur. Nearly wettin' meself with excitement.

And, later on, him taking me hand and leading me into an alley.

I didn't know he was a courier then, didn't care. He's so proud of that shagging job. Never shuts up about it. Just scooting here and there, with parcels and things, but he thinks he's Evel Knievel. You couldn't say that to him, though.

It was when we were in bed last night that he started on about us having a huge feed of the horrid fish. We were after doing it at the time and I was pretending to be happy although I was nearer to crying. He'd been so rough and quick, driving it in and me all dry. Going so hard me head was banging off the board. I had to close me eyes because his face was so strange and twisted, like an ugly mask. I didn't tell him he was hurting me, I knew he wouldn't stop. When he finally shot his load, it felt horrible. Dirty. He stayed on top of me for ages, all quiet, heavy as a rock. I was afraid to push him off, afraid he'd see the truth in me opened eyes.

No wonder I had bad dreams later. About the lake and that. The stones.

I hoped he'd be in too much of a panic in the morning to think about the fish – but no. Straight into it he went, even before he was fully dressed.

Telling me how to chop off the head, and slice the belly open, and be sure to get all the gutty bits out. Me mind started to spin the more he went on and on; the bed felt shaky under me, as if the whole gaff was collapsing.

I imagined the fish jumping again and the blood on Johnny's hands after he dug out the hook. I even heard the cries of the white bird as she left the lake and flew off like the clappers.

And then, what really freaked me, he held out his flick knife.

'Here,' he said, 'I'll leave ya me blade for the cutting.'

It felt so cold as I took it from him. So dangerous. Everything suddenly went dead quiet, not a sound of cars or buses or nothing from outside. The bleeding city seemed to have stopped.

I dropped the knife the second he swaggered off out the door, off to his big important courier crap. Me heart was flying like the frightened bird.

I can't do it, I just can't fucking do it. God knows what'd spill out if I opened him. Shit, I feel sick again. Could I be . . .? No, it's just the fish that's making me sick. That's all, just the shagging fish.

Let Johnny do the cutting if he wants. And the frying too. And he better not expect me to eat any because I won't. Don't want to be pukin' me guts out, maybe have me insides swell up like a balloon.

Johnny, com'ere till I tell ya …

Listen, Johnny, I was over in me Ma's …

I couldn't get the knife open, Johnny …

The Prefect

The November fair of that year brought a glut of cattle to the village of Hillstown. Fodder was scarce because of the wet summer; winter pushed in early and with a vengeance. Prices would be bad, it was feared. A case of pocketing what you could, and making do.

The late arrivals got no farther than Mick Tobin's forge on one side of the village, and the priest's ivy-coated residence on the other. If ever a fair was made for the tan-booted dealers it was this one, their wallets of blue notes guaranteed to reap rich dividend. The tanglers, too, would make hay; come noon they'd search out the most vulnerable, and pounce – leaving many a man to wander homewards with an uneasy mind. Stock let go for small money, maybe the censure of a wife to face.

Or just the four walls.

It was a day to look sharp, a day to avoid the bars.

Packie Muldoon left his Raleigh bicycle in the yard at the back of Burke's bar and grocery, adjusted his Sunday cap, and hobbled out into the raucous heart of the fair. He felt in top form, knowing he was one of the few who could hold what he had. Men were feeling the pinch, the best of yearlings would be on show. He'd buy, if the money was right. He melted into the throng. A casual hand stealing along beefy flanks, his ear tuned to the offers of the dealers.

He was from out Dooach way, a bachelor by inclination and circumstance – the latter being the more irrevocable condition. Though just turned sixty-one, he bore the mark of a man well into his seventies. A gammy leg didn't help, the result of a quarry accident in his youth.

His farm, alone, people might envy. The house hadn't seen a lick of paint in years, a bleak sight indeed, but the plains of dry land surrounding it were second to none. Aberdeen Angus were fattened on those rich acres until they were ready for the butcher's knife; the fat cheque went straight into the bank in Creeve. The income from the few pigs he kept more than covered his frugal wants.

It wasn't much of a life but it was the only life he knew. At least I'll never go short, he could comfort himself. For men of his type, that had to be, and was, enough. But a quick look round his remote holding said there was money there, serious money.

Around two o'clock he decided to get in off the streets and treat himself to a rare drink. A drop of whiskey would be grand, warm his blood for the cycle back to Dooach. Earlier, he'd given consideration to a pair of rangy shorthorns but, as he entered into tentative negotiations with the seller, a few dodgy-looking boyos stuck their noses in and the cautious Packie cut his stick. Several times after, he saw the same skulduggery over the same bullocks. Them blasted tanglers, he thought. A pure dread.

A dozen or so men ranged along Teddy Burke's counter, pints of stout and hot whiskey in front of them. Talk was specific and muted. The bad prices were mourned all round, Packie Muldoon loudest of all in the lamentations. As the complaints grew louder his small Paddy tasted extra sweet, so much so that he ordered a second one. He'd still be home in good time, just had to make sure he didn't forget to collect his boots.

When he finally slid off his stool, after a third Paddy, and hobbled out the back to his Raleigh, his heart was light with contentment. There was something in the oul' drink all the same. Definite.

As he walked the steep hill that curved towards Mulgrew's cottage he found himself thinking of Katie. He'd seen her in the morning, when leaving his boots in, and she seemed in fair enough form.

Recently, the cobbler's daughter had become the subject of broad rumour. It was said that a great change had come over her, and not for the better. Even Packie, a man who lived alone in the back of beyond, had heard talk. For he, too, had to buy grub; and Tilly Kelly's shop was the place to find out who was who and what was what. The previous Friday he'd been in there, and a nest of women were clucking within earshot. Ahhh, the poor thing is turning a shade queer. Should have got out more but 'twasn't aisy for her, I suppose. No. No. God bless the mark! Madge Benson came in and settled, said she heard Katie was trucking round with some buck from over Creeve direction. Some buck from Creeve! Didn't I often say there was more to that lady than met the eye. It's the quiet ones you want to watch. Oh there's a history there if you travel back far enough. Ohhh, I could tell it but I'm not one for gabbing. Less said easiest mended.

Packie kept his own counsel. If he hadn't the good word to say he'd say nothing.

But he heard the words *she's trucking, she's trucking with a buck from over Creeve direction* as he neared the gate and saw Katie stooped by the side of the porch, pruning the rosebush which always flourished in that suntrap corner.

The whiskey had made him game for chat.

'Hardy evening, Miss Mulgrew!' he cried, parking his Raleigh against the whitewashed wall and squirming his shoulders.

Katie straightened. She regarded him for a mute moment, then said: 'It's cold surely. Looking like frost.'

'Definite.' A pause. 'Wonder would me oul' boots be fixed?'

'They should be, or near it.'

'Sound, sound.' He looked back down towards the village and squeezed his bulbous nose. 'Fierce drove of cattle out today. Never seen the like.'

'We saw them passing.'

'Bad prices. Men giving them away.'

'Mmmm.'

'Aye, that's it.' He leant easily on the wall and studied the neat beds. 'You're a dab hand in the garden,' he said. 'I often stopped to look at your flowers, never seen nicer.'

She dipped her eyes, suddenly awkward as a twelve-year-old.

'I mean in the summer,' he added, 'when they'd be blooming.'

'Come on in,' she muttered, 'and we'll see about your boots.'

'Oh aye-aye, me boots.'

Packie followed her in along the flagged path.

Jack was still busy with the rasp, and the tacks had yet to be driven, so Packie Muldoon was obliged to wait for a while. He sat. The kitchen was so cosy and neat, the trace of a woman's hand in every corner, he soon began to feel uneasy. He might have carried the smells of the fair in with him, cakes of dung on his soles. No stone floors here – the grandest of lino.

'Make the man a cup of tea,' said Jack, rasping all the while. 'I'm sure you could do with a mouthful, Packie.'

'Just a quick drop in the hand.'

Though Packie's eye had avoided her since he'd come in, she'd sensed he was thinking about her; now, as she reached to get the tea canister off the mantelpiece, she sensed his bowed gaze on her.

'Mighty turnout of cattle, Jack,' Packie said then, his head kicking round to the cobbler.

'There would, there would,' said Jack absently, slipping a boot over the tongue of the last and bending for his bag of tacks.

'But bad prices.'

'Is that right?'

'Shocking.'

'Oh.'

'Men giving them away.'

'Now.'

The hammer sang a horseshoe of tacks into the mirror-smooth leather.

'Sit in.' Katie's tone, strangely intimate, erased Packie's unease.

He swept his cap off as he rose. 'Good girl,' he muttered.

'Daddy, will you have a mug?'

'Work away, work away.'

Outside, a lone heifer was being planted homewards, her lows carrying on the still air as she called for her sold kin.

'Can't you take a bun?'

'Ah no, I'm all right.'

'Go on, I made them myself.'

'You did not!' Packie's upper body swung round to where Katie sat by the range knitting. She blushed. He turned away slowly.

'Lovely,' he said.

The hammer went silent finally and Jack Mulgrew eyed the finished job. His sausage fingers fondled the true edges of the soles, the cool half-moon heads of the shiny tacks. 'Ya might knock another few winters outa them, Packie,' he said, rising stiffly from his bench. 'Th'uppers are sound.'

'Good man.' Packie swallowed the last of his third bun and made to rise.

'Stay where y'are, can't ya?'

'Ah begod no, I'll go, Jack. Ya don't find the night.'

'Go on, drink up that tea first.'

Packie, caught in a limbo between standing and sitting, reclaimed his seat in slow motion. 'A grand drop it is,' he mused. 'And nice buns, too.'

'Ya hear that, girl?' said Jack. She looked up, her lips kinking into the faintest of smiles. Jack nodded, a nod so slight it could have been read as encouragement or the heavy acceptance of immutable things. He then offered a match to his pipe and turned away, a halo of smoke soon about his head.

Only a single bun remained on the willow-pattern plate when Packie rose.

'Thanks very much, Katie,' he said, his words sounding comically solemn. She smiled in her shy fashion, acutely aware of his having used her Christian name.

''Twas nothing,' she said, her eyes dipping.

'Now, sir! What do I owe ya?'

'Examine them first, can't ya,' said Jack. 'See if you're satisfied.'

This was a standard line of old Jack's – almost as if, in a childlike way, he craved praise. Packie lifted his boots from the workbench, wore them as gloves, and clapped the tacked soles together.

'A noble job,' he said.

'Give me fifteen bob so.' Jack moved to busy himself at his bench as he spoke, a man never at ease when it came to bargaining.

Packie coaxed a wad of money from an inside pocket, enough to buy six or seven cattle. He isolated two ten-shilling notes and considered them for a moment. 'Here,' he said then, nudging Jack, claiming Jack's arm, secreting the notes into his hand. 'Close your fist on that.'

Jack checked the money. 'Come 'ere, Packie, have you nothing smaller?'

'Take it, you've it well earned.'

'I can't do that.'

'Those boots are better than the new thing.'

'Right,' yielded Jack finally, 'I'll take it but you'll take a bit back, if it's only for the luck of the thing. Wait there now and don't stir till I come up.' He shuffled away to the lower bedroom and eased the door shut. He cocked his ear close to the woodwormed panels. Silence; then the croaky drone of Packie. Jack, hard of hearing, had to make do with his imaginings. He shifted from the door, sighed, and absently scratched his head. He lifted the statue of the Virgin off the mantelpiece, jigged it until the purse slipped from its hollow interior. He drew out a single half-crown; he fingered its chilly smoothness, wondering still what was being said in the kitchen, then went back up.

'Now, Packie, put that in your pocket.'

'Oh aye, sound.' Packie, seeming befuddled, turned sharply for the door.

'Your boots!' said Jack. 'Bechrist don't be going off without them!' He eyed his daughter as he spoke, anxious to draw her into that light-hearted moment. She upped from her chair and hovered by the range.

'I had an oul' box for them,' said Packie, scanning without any focus, 'somewhere.'

'It's there, under the bench,' said Katie.

'That's the very one.'

Jack moved to the turf bin and clawed out a few sods. 'Fire's gone down,' he muttered.

'I'll go, in the name of God,' he heard Packie say.

'Good luck, Packie,' he replied, not turning his head.

A minute or so later Katie came back in, having seen Packie Muldoon off.

Whatever was said or dreamt of on that November evening, however tentative their initial stirrings, Katie and Packie would go on to court – after a fashion – and become man and wife less than four months later. She was pushing forty. Her future and hopes were knowable to none.

The marriage was the talk of Hillstown. Such a rare pair, and so sudden. The fact of them opting for the chapel in Creeve – a good eight miles away – and inviting not a single neighbour, meant they were wed, and settled in remote Dooach, before a soul heard. This secretive aspect of their doings, while understandable, didn't go down well in certain quarters. Muldoon was tight, the bastard wouldn't fork out for a do. The more sentimental of the village's womenfolk simply wished they'd been given the opportunity to see Katie on her big day. She must have made a lovely bride.

She was one nice lassie, she was topping. Yes, she took after her father. God love her, he kept her to himself too long. It's not natural. It was nothing less than a sin she never took up with someone. Hadn't the chance.

But now, I ask you, The Limp Muldoon, of all people. Who'd think it? And how did they keep the thing so quiet? Beats Banagher, Madge. I knew it, I knew something was up. That time Lizzie met the *cailín* in the post office she said she was like a hen on eggs. Of course, soft Lizzie thought she was just gone a bit queer, felt sympathy for her. Queer me eye! She got the whiff of money and jumped at it. Oul' Jack, I saw him without a knee in his breeches. That's the good truth, the same man got nothing soft. You'll see, though, herself won't be slow lightening the miser's wallet. Good luck to her. Still, they're well met all the same.

For every crooked foot there's a crooked shoe. Stop it, Madge, that's not right. O, it might all turn out better than we think. Lord, aren't people a sight. Now, you're talking. A pure sight.

The Sabbath was the day to observe them. The lure of their first arrival at the chapel gates as a couple had proven tempting indeed, and few missed it. It was normal for the menfolk to huddle along the wall, smoking pipes or strong cigarettes, chatting away the last few minutes before the altar boy swung gongs from the heavy bell. A few women joined them that morning.

A silence fell as Packie and Katie rounded into view; elbows nudged, all eyes found focus. They surely made a strange pair, and the passage of time would not alter this view. Her wifely status seemed to have given Katie a fresh confidence and she was all smiles as the well-wishers left the wall, hands outstretched. She wore a new tweed coat, her hair was newly done, she looked smashing. Packie was the same as ever, his wardrobe obviously unadded to. He grinned, though, grinned through it all.

A sunny Sunday in March and, as usual, the early Mass-goers ranged along the wall.

'Begod we have strangers this morning,' said Hughie Curley, he being the first to spot the approach of the mystery car. Visitors, most would have assumed. Swanks home from England.

Hands rose against the frosty light.

Mute wondering gave way to open-mouthed amazement when the Ford Prefect drew up alongside the wall, idled for a moment, and then reversed smoothly into the sanded parking space.

'Bejazus if it's not the Muldoons,' someone muttered.

There they were, cocooned within that brand-new motor car, Katie at the wheel, Packie by her side, the cobbler Mulgrew in the back. They sat tight for a few minutes, savouring their moment – or maybe feeling ill at ease, wilting under the gaze of village scrutiny. The mutterings. Well, if that doesn't take the biscuit. And the way herself is able to manage. She can handle it. Begod that cost money. Now you're talking, Bob. A four-door. Aye, the real McCoy. The man inside won't be pleased, that's a better-looking motor than his own. The priest? The priest. Oh, dear! And look at the cut of himself in the front, he's like a – Quit, they're getting out! Watch this! Stand back!

Greetings were muted as they crossed to the silvery gates, Katie leading the way with a confident step. Curt nods; a 'grand morning' chorus from a few; a few hands rising in token salute. Packie's grin was full and fixed; it seemed to say to all and sundry: 'See now what money can buy, hah!' Old Jack alone revealed, by the slight hang of his head, that maybe he wished to distance himself from such a big show.

Katie Muldoon, as far as anyone knew, tasted her first drop of alcohol in Teddy Burke's premises one Friday afternoon. Nothing too alarming, just a quiet glass of stout after she did her weekly shopping. Yet the tongues weren't slow to wag. A woman didn't venture into a bar alone in the Hillstowns of the time, especially not a married woman with plenty to do at home. And she dallied a long time over that single drink. Sat over by the fireplace for maybe an hour while Teddy the publican kept his head low in the pages of the *Anglo-Celt*, and The Red Langan – his only other customer – sucked his sixth pint of the day.

She was about twenty months married then and it had already become plain that something was up. Maybe an addition was on the way? Maybe she was just lonely, only the rooks to keep her company out there in Dooach? Or maybe Packie was driving her up the walls, a man never used to a woman kind? The Sunday watchers had as many answers as questions but all they could do was silently wish her well. She wouldn't be one for accepting advice or help. Stay out of it, let her soldier on.

Jack Mulgrew no longer took a seat to Mass in the Prefect. Strict in his devotion, he always liked to be in the chapel in good time, claim his seat near the rail. The motorized pair cut it far too fine.

Soon, the Prefect became a familiar fixture in Teddy Burke's yard. Katie gave Fridays a miss now, seeming to prefer the quieter, mid-week days.

Christmas neared; her drinking continued; she'd become 'a pure scandal'. And yet, come Christmas morning, she marched confidently past the crowded wall, her face pale but proud, eau-de-Cologne lingering in her wake like a challenge.

Packie Muldoon now began to elicit a certain sympathy. While previously the general view was that he got what he deserved – a woman who was threatening to blow his miser horde to the four winds – the tide had gradually turned. Katie was going too far. 'Tisn't right, she's turning the poor fella into a laughing stock. But how is he putting up with it, giving her such liberty?

A mystery, no less.

On the other hand a course it's only natural, the poor woman wanting to get out. Looking at that hoor all day. Oh aye, plain natural. Course, there'd be a hunger in her, Mick. The oul' bunk is a job for a young buck. And he'd want to be in his health. Definite. All joking aside, I suppose she would be kinda chancy when the porter is in. Now you're talking. And he wouldn't have to cross a ditch either, you could bull cows in the back of that motor car.

Stop! Stop!

Aye, let the hare sit.

Whether or not she was aware of the gossip, Katie continued to frequent Burke's bar. She was well over a year going in there now, yet not once did Teddy try to engage her in chat. The few words, that was all. He knew when to talk and when not to talk; Katie was the type to leave alone. He did worry about her, though. Driving home in that powerful car, in the pitch-dark more often than not, it was enough to concern any man. But she always seemed to walk out sober and straight – 'Too sober, if you know what I mean.'

A few stragglers from the other bars would often drift into Burke's when the Prefect was about: lone men, half drunk and wondering. None was ever bold enough to occupy a seat by the fireplace; Katie's stoical, distracted attitude encouraged no slobbering chancers.

The grocery section of Burke's also lured a few extra customers. Scarfed and solid citizens would comb the shelves nearest the bar, eyes peeled for the wayward wife. They were always disappointed because, while the bar area was open to the shop, the spot where Katie sat with her cares was maddeningly out of view. And they got no joy from Maggie either, Teddy's soft-spoken missus, who met the most oblique of queries with a look that would curdle milk.

There was no stopping the gossip, though.

When the Prefect rolled through Hillstown the village hummed with the expectancy of some momentous scandal: Katie'll get into trouble yet; she'll bring the wrath of the priest down on top of her, hot and heavy; it's not right; someone should tell him; one of these fine days Packie will lose the head and barge into Burke's, pull her out like a dog.

One Thursday evening, after leaving Burke's fireplace, Katie wandered through to the grocery section. She didn't seem at all certain of her needs, picking apparently at random from the cluttered shelves. A slab of jelly, louse powder, a packet of sweets, lard, aspirin, a tin of beans. She smiled vacantly as she dumped all on the patch of bare counter.

'Very cold evening, Missis Muldoon,' said Maggie, licking her stub of pencil before totting up on a scrap of brown wrapping paper.

'There was something else I wanted,' Katie muttered absently.

She turned away as if she hadn't heard herself being addressed. She again scanned the shelves; her index finger roaming, unfocused, trying to spear some elusive item. Maggie observed her with growing concern.

'Nutmeg!' she cried, spinning round. 'I'm looking for nutmeg.'

Maggie shook her head heavily. 'I'm sorry,' she said, 'we don't stock it at all. I'm sorry.'

'Nutmeg! But you must have nutmeg!'

'Sure if I had it I'd give it to you, and gladly.'

'But I want to bake a cake, a sweet cake.' There was an edge of desperation in Katie's tone; her teeth dug ino her lip, as though she were stifling a childhood sob.

'Maybe you could try Kelly's?' offered Maggie. Her eyes dipped away into the counter. 'I'm so sorry now.'

Katie scrunched her hands into paled fists, her breathing became a rasp; she made for the door, her few pathetic groceries left behind.

Teddy emerged from the back bar.

'Did you hear that?' Maggie asked him.

'I did. The poor creature.'

Katie didn't appear in Burke's again for five whole weeks. It was said, in the meantime, that the Prefect was spotted at The Sailor's Rest in Creeve, or then again parked on the Glan road with her ladyship asleep inside, down a lane at an ungodly hour of the night.

When she did return, Teddy was quick to put up a free drink for her. No big drama, just his way of saying what he couldn't find words for.

It was a Tuesday and there wasn't another soul on the premises. She took her drink at the counter and gulped it. She shyly asked for another before claiming her usual armchair by the fireplace. She gazed into the empty hearth, too early for a fire to be lit, nothing in its grate save a spent Players packet and matchbox, tossed in there by someone passing through.

She was on her sixth bottle when the street door moaned open and Freddy Dolan sloped in. His demeanour said he was well cut, as usual.

'Gimme a small one there, Teddy.' A muted quality to his voice, the tone of a man testing the waters. 'Powers,' he qualified, but Teddy was already pouring the correct spirit.

Dolan was around thirty and a bit of a lone wolf. Tending to be contrary sometimes in drink he wasn't exactly welcome in Teddy Burke's, but he knew this and thus rarely lingered.

He tipped a spatter of water into his whiskey, a peripheral eye focusing on Katie. He lit a Woodbine and turned full towards her as he breathed out the match. He downed some of his whiskey; his free hand closed round coins in the well of his pocket. He kept looking at her, having had enough drink on board to become brazen – if only in thought. He flicked ash off his smoke.

Katie cupped her tulip glass in her lap, hunched under the weight of her thoughts. Teddy seemed immersed in his paper, yet the moment Dolan moved to cross the flags he said: 'Freddy, come on. Drink up your whiskey and be quiet.'

'Sshh,' said Dolan, sweeping an arm backwards. 'I'm only going over to spake to the woman. You don't mind, missis, do you?'

Katie just stared blankly at him; this he grasped as licence to sit.

After a few minutes, during which not a single word crossed the hearth, he upped and returned to the counter. 'Two Powers, Teddy, good man.'

'She doesn't want any of your whiskey,' said Teddy testily.

'It's all right, boss, the job is sound.'

'Stand there where y'are and –'

'I'll take it,' Katie cut in. Both men glanced at her, as if she were a being hitherto incapable of speech. Dolan turned back and grinned slyly at Teddy. Teddy slapped his paper shut and rose to fill the glasses.

Two hours later the pair headed for the door. Katie's step was less than sure; Dolan, too, was showing wear. The Prefect revved long and loud then eventually it sailed off down the street and broke left for Glan.

Dolan showed a few times with Katie over the following week but whatever novelty or comfort he extracted from her company soon wore off. He cut his stick, left her to plough a lone and lonely furrow.

Gone, too, were the bottles of porter. Whiskey was now her tipple. She abandoned the fireplace, took to hiding away in the poky snug. Wainscotted walls, a picture of a girl with a red setter on one of them; a hatch giving onto the counter.

The Prefect stayed away from the chapel one wet Sunday, Packie having to brave it on his resurrected Raleigh. The next Sunday the same. People bled for him.

There were those who believed that Father O'Dea paid a visit to the grey house in Dooach, but, if he did, the success of his mission was to prove limited. Katie would return to the fold, but only the odd Sunday, always arriving late and alone, sneaking into a back pew to avoid her father. She never headed up to receive any more and was the first away at the end.

The porch boys said she was in the shakes, failed beyond belief.

The car, too, showed damage. Scrapes along the sides, a headlight gone, an ugly dent in the left wing.

The first Tuesday in November, 1963. Four years, almost to the day, since Packie Muldoon ate raisin buns at Katie Mulgrew's table. All Soul's Day, Mass in the chapel, a fair again on the streets.

It was a fine crisp day, sunny for the most part, but a whisper of sleet clung to the air. The turnout of cattle was unusually small because winter feed was plentiful in every man's haggard. Culled and stringy yearlings, mostly, animals hardly worth giving good hay to. Tangler stock.

Come early afternoon, women were out scouring their doorsteps, flashing buckets of water: a monthly ritual. Madge Benson leant on her brush as her neighbour from a few doors along, Mary McFadden, nosed up. They exchanged the briefest of preliminaries before entering the main topic.

'She's in again,' Madge nodded to the car in Burke's yard.

'I saw her landing. Hours ago.'

'Isn't it a sight. You wouldn't know how a body sticks it.'

'No. She made early Mass, all the same. Brought himself, too.'

'Must've just jaunted him home and turned round.'

'God help her,' sighed Mary. 'She's a pity.'

'A pity is the word.'

'Stuck in there for the whole evening now.'

'Oh aye, the whole blessed evening.'

Madge lifted her brush and readied to lash out as a few dung-caked Angus loped homewards. Then she looked to where the bonnet of the Prefect glistened under the gunmetal November sky.

'Anyone inside with her, I wonder?'

'Oh, don't be talking.'

'Buying her drink, maybe.'

'That too.'

'Driving the fool further.'

'Don't you know well.'

'Bad luck to them anyway, it's not right.'

'No, oh no, but sure what can anyone do?'

'You'll find the man at home is in a queer tangle.'

'He didn't know how well off he was. He knows now.'

'Ahhh, God help the people.'

'Aye indeed, God save everyone.'

It was about ten when Katie Muldoon emerged from Burke's. She had company, a porter-bellied tangler by the name of Lally. He winged an arm round her, gripped an ash-plant under his oxter; his hat sat well back on his bullish head. She seemed waif-like beside him.

The street was hushed in the grip of frost, the smallest sound carried.

Madge Benson left her novena aside, took off her reading glasses. Up and over to the window, up with a corner of lace curtain.

The two shadowy figures had turned into Burke's yard. They veered apart, came together again. Several times they did this, almost as if involved in an absurd dance. The wash of the full moon on them, the Prefect hulking in the blackened lee of the bar's gable.

Once more they came together; this time their union held.

For a shocking second, Madge thought they were going at it there in the very yard, but then she heard a moaned Nooo! from Katie and saw her arcing hand whip across the tangler's jaw.

'Jesus Mary and Joseph,' Madge muttered.

Lally searched about for his dropped plant, found it, fired a few parting curses at Katie and staggered off in the direction of Mick Joe Bell's.

The tracks of his boots rang on stone. A dog broke into barking.

Katie steered towards the Prefect, sank leaden arms onto its roof. Madge imagined the poor thing was crying but if she was the dog was drowning her out. She stayed slouched against the car for a good five minutes, then she pulled the door open and the interior lit up. She didn't get in, not yet. She leant on the door. Madge could now see her clearly: her head hung low, one of her arms drooped over the edge, bisecting the iced window.

'Oh Jesus above, let someone come,' she pleaded. No one came. Katie got into the car, shut the door: darkness swallowed her.

The cold engine turned and turned before finally growling to life. The headlights flicked on, off, on again. Exhaust fumes wafted across the maw of the yard. A final, prolonged rev and she was off.

Andy McGuinn was out at the crack of dawn, a backload of sweet hay bending him as he made his way across the triangular bottom. Five beef shorthorns loped to meet him, lowing in welcome. He divided the feed into even piles, talked to his quiet cattle and scratched their rumps. Turning back for the house, a glint over in the corner of the field drew his eye. He raised his palm, visored it against the icy sun. He shuffled forward and soon he was muttering in dread. A car had come off the road, dived into the drop which was known locally as Branley's Hollow. Fifty yards from the scene he swung away to alert help. It was Muldoon's Prefect: he'd know that car anywhere.

In less than an hour a crowd had gathered, still more hurrying along the backroads and over the crunchy fields.

Silence and dipped heads, Woodbine smoke wisping from cupped hands.

Father O'Dea pulled up in his little Austin. He wore the stole, for last rites would surely have to be administered here.

Two tractors tut-tut-tutted in waiting as the heavy chains were attached down below by Mike Lawlor and Paudge McElweeny. A snot-nosed youth ducked in for a peep; his father's hand yanked him back. Diesel fumes saturated the stilled air.

The priest offered what comfort he could to Packie and then edged across to Jack Mulgrew. He clasped the cobbler's hand, and moved on. Down in the Hollow Mike Lawlor stifled a curse as a stout thorn dug along his wrist. Paudge McElweeny, too, was suffering down there in the briars and bushes.

Two neighbours of Packie's pushed in and flanked him with silence. Words were redundant, they made do with weighty nods.

The first stirring of the tractors caused an involuntary movement in the crowd. Necks were craned, all eyes fast on the rim of the drop. The chains went taut; the bald tyres spun smoke from the front, then gained purchase. The dreadful inching forward began. Paudge McElweeny directed the operation – cool as always, a man made for such days. A warning shout from the side as one of the chains slipped on the drawbar. Forward, forward, slow but sure.

'They're bringing her,' someone muttered.

One more minute and the tail of the Prefect appeared over the edge with hardly a trace of fresh damage on it. The wickedness of the early sun had melted most of the frost from the windows, yet no figure was visible inside.

Nobody moved to check.

Then Paudge McElweeny hopped off his tractor and tossed a Woodbine butt aside as he strode along his chains. He signalled quietly, meaningfully, for the priest. Those who wore caps or hats swept them off.

Katie's upper body pitched out as the jammed door was yanked open. Gentle but firm arms pinned Jack Mulgrew to his spot.

The new year, January a month of few favours. Hillstown's streets as drab as they had ever been. Out in the hills, farmers worrying about hay, despite their full haggards. A long time till May day. Spare it.

Packie Muldoon went about his business in a more or less normal fashion. His bullocks, fed with bull nuts, piled on the weight; his house reverted to a quiet that seemed destined to be its true state. The Prefect stayed at the back of the hayshed, where Paudge McElweeny left it, never to visit a road again. It would rot there in time, but first Packie removed its spongy red-leather front seats and placed them either side of his hearth.

He did it naturally and without guilt.

They were great seats.

Nights he'd sit on the passenger side of the fire in his hushed house. It was like Katie had gone out for something. He was in the car waiting. Soon she'd return and slip into the empty driver's seat, let down the handbrake and take them away somewhere out of this.